William Wallbeck

Fables - Ancient and Modern

After the Manner of La Fontaine

William Wallbeck

Fables - Ancient and Modern
After the Manner of La Fontaine

ISBN/EAN: 9783744768214

Printed in Europe, USA, Canada, Australia, Japan

Cover: Foto ©Andreas Hilbeck / pixelio.de

More available books at **www.hansebooks.com**

F A B L E S;

ANCIENT and MODERN:

AFTER THE MANNER OF

L A F O N T A I N E.

B Y

WILLIAM WALLBECK.

FLORIFERIS UT APES IN SALTIBUS OMNIA LIBANT,
OMNIA NOS ITIDEM DEPASCIMUR AUREA DICTA,
AUREA, PERPETUA SEMPER DIGNISSIMA VITA.

L O N D O N:

PRINTED FOR THE AUTHOR:

AND SOLD BY

R. FAULDER; J. STOCKDALE; J. DEBRETT; J. EDWARDS;
J. WALTER; and E. NEWBERRY.

PRICE, *THREE SHILLINGS AND SIX-PENCE,* SEWED,

M,DCC,LXXXVII,

Lately pupliſhed, by the ſame Author,

THE LIFE OF CERVANTES,

In ſmall Octavo, Price One Shilling.

AND

SOCRATES AND XANTIPPE,

A BURLESQUE TALE,

. *In Quarto*, Price Two Shillings.

D E D I C A T I O N.

T O

R I C H A R D W O O D E S O N,

Vinerian Professor of the Laws
of England. (Oxford.)

S I R.

To endeavour at *imitating* LAFONTAINE, to whom fo many good judges have afcribed excellence *above imitation,* will be thought (whatever apologies I may have to offer) highly temerarious. But, how much have I added to that temerity, by fetting your Name at the head of this Dedication! — Thereby obtruding an imperfect Work upon the notice of fo able a Critic: — of one converfant with the living languages, as well as the dead; and competent to compare thefe my Fables with thofe of the Great Mafters. How much mine muft fuffer by the comparifon, I am well aware. But, acute as is your penetration, and correct your tafte, I am lefs afraid of the fcrutiny than they would be who know you only in your literary capacity; as a Profeffor, and a Scholar.

I am

I am under lefs alarm, becaufe I am acquainted as well with the goodnefs of your heart, as the ftrength of your head. Severity of Judgement, I know, will be attempered by the gentlenefs of Candour.

" *Summum jus, fumma injuria:*" — is a maxim which holds as good in Critifcim, as in Law. He muft be liberal, as well as learned, who is qualified to fit in either Court. " *Ufe every Man after his defert, and who fhall efcape whipping?*"—Not I;— finner as I am. No; nor even HAYLEY himfelf; who in fome of his Works approaches as near perfection, as humaniry can do : but if no offences were to be paffed over, the Beadles of Parnaffus would have lafhed him long ago.

What HORACE has faid of Man himfelf, may very well be applied to his Compofitions.

—Vitiis nemo fine nafcitur : optimus ille eft
Qui minimis urgetur.

Millions of Men have been writing for thoufands of years; and there never yet came from the Prefs one faultlefs Work.—Nor, probably, ever will. For,— if, under the pains and penalties of Sin, the enthufiafm of Virtue, and the certain rewards of Religion, Man is incapable of attaining to Perfection in his moral capacity,—it would be abfurd to expect fupreme excellence from him as an Author. Unlefs, indeed, we are to fuppofe that *Poetry* is more animating than Virtue;

that

that the *Critics'* Damnation is more terrible than the Wrath of GOD; that our paffion for *fame* is more ardent than our zeal for Religion; and that our *temporal Intereft* is more dear to us than our eternal Happinefs.

As far as thefe ought to influence any one, they do me. I hope to reap *Profit* from my Lucubrations,— becaufe I have occafion for money. For *Fame* I avow myfelf a Candidate; though my friends tell me I am a wretched canvaffer: for I make my pretenfions with a confidence fure to give offence to little minds. I am forry for it. I would not feem arrogant: but I cannot at all times check the ardour of an afpiring fpirit. As to the common tricks, the low, bafe arts of electioneering, I fcorn to practife them. I know not how to flatter:

Or crook the pregnant hinges of the knee,
Where thrift may follow fawning.

I cannot wheedle; and I will not bribe.

Making public thefe principles is not the way to gain over to my fide the majority of Voters. Well, then; I will be content with the Voices of thofe only, whofe patronage is fufficient honour.

And here, not impertinently, I beg leave to make my acknowledgements to that learned, and refpectable Corps of Journalifts, the CRITICAL REVIEWERS, who

who were pleafed to fpeak fo very handfomely of both my former Publications. (*)

Although I cannot meanly ftoop to fue for favours, no one has a more grateful fenfe of obligations con-ferred. And, the greateft 'obligation,—indeed, the only one that can properly be conferred on Authors,— and the greateft,—indeed, the only fervice the Jour-nalifts can do to Literature, is by full, fair, candid, and impartial Criticifm. Such every Writer not in-toxicated with vanity muft wifh for. For my own part, I can fay with great fincerity,

Verum amo, verum mihi dicite de me.

It would ill become me to appreciate refpectively the Works of the Public Critics, were I ever fo well acquainted with them : but, in truth, there are fome I know only by their Advertifements. Such as fall in my way (at the diftance I am from the Metropolis) I perufe with the curiofity natural to an Author ;— but not of one *tremblingly alive all o'er.* Happily, I am not of a timid nature. Should a Drawcanfir, diftort his angry phiz at me, cock his Kevenhuller Hat,

---

* Of the one, The Life of Cervantes, the account is too long to infert here; highly flattering as it is : I therefore refer the Reader to the Critical Review, for Auguft 1785.

Of the other, Socrates and Xantippe, I fhall have occafion to fpeak prefently; but for a full account, I alfo refer the Reader to the faid Review, for March 1786.

Hat, lay his hand upon his fword, and thunder out an artillery of oaths, loud enough to break the drum of a nervous man's ears,—I could behold, and hear him perfeƈtly compofed. Should the Pope, in his holy wrath, anathematize me for a Heretic; and curfe me as oft and *pioufly* as Dr. SLOP did OBADIAH,— I fhould liften to him, not with the emotion of anger, but of pity;—of regret that the imbecility of the human mind is fuch, as to miftake the fuggeftions of Diabolifm, for the impulfe of Religion.

Should a Pfeudo-Critic—(I have now got to the depth of my anticlimax)—Should a Pfeudo-Critic, glancing his eye over the Title Page, exclaim, with peevifh wit, " *O, Imitatores ! fervum pecus:*"—Then, reading one fhort Fable, condemn all as execrable ;— I fhould be little hurt ; and lefs furprifed at it : for I have often feen fuch Men of *intuitive* genius, rummaging over a Bookfeller's Counter, and paffing judgment upon a dozen New Pamphlets, in about as many minutes.

Thefe fuperficial, mock Critics, remind me of a *Farrier*, whom I would fain have perfuaded to adminifter *James's Powder* to a fick horfe of mine. "' No, no : Mafter. There is not enough in that "' Paper to do any good. Befides I don't like the "' *colour* of it."'—' The colour! Friend. Do you ' judge of medicines by the eye only ? Do you never
' *analyze*

' *analyze* them ?' '"" No; never: Sir.—If you catch
"" me telling *any lies*, I'll cure your horfe for nothing.'"

Excufe the digreſſion, and the *pun*, too; which is
almoſt bad enough to be a good one.

They, however, who condemn a Book *in toto*, are
not an Author's worſt enemies; becaufe their opinions
have weight only with felf-confeſſed Blockheads, who
are content to pin their faith upon another's ſleeve.
Or, as IAGO ſays,

- *Who will as tenderly be led by the noſe*
As Aſſes are.

The moſt formidable are thofe, who, from innate
bafenefs of foul, or from rivalry, or jealoufy, or the
jarring intereſts of Bookfellers, fet down to fcrutinize
a Work with *malice prepenfe*; refolved, at any rate,
to pick a quarrel with, and tear to pieces the poor
Author laying at their mercy.

How poſſible it is to pull to pieces even thofe ſtrongeſt
in fame, every one muſt know, who has read JOHN-
SON's *Criticifms* on the *Epitaphs* written by POPE.
The juſtnefs of thofe Criticifms it is not my purpofe
to difpute. Like every thing that came from JOHN-
SON, they ſhow the hand of a great Maſter: at once
evincing that clearnefs of comprehenfion, that ſhrewd-
nefs of intellect, and folidity of judgement, by which
he was fo eminently diſtinguiſhed: and which, ex-
preſſed in well-chofen words, artificially, yet happily
arranged,

arranged, formed a language fingularly pleafing, and peculiarly his own; being at the fame time fmooth and energetic; not too copious, nor too concife. So that Dr. Johnson,—whether he was or was not the very beft claffic Scholar of his day,—was certainly the very beft didactic Writer.

Neverthelefs, (to go back to the fubject,) I muft fay, the Doctor's Criticifms upon Pope's Epitaphs are not to be reckoned amongft the beft efforts of his genius. The remarks are none of them trite, but fome are trivial; and, upon the whole, they look fo like *Criticifm* in the common and worft acceptation of the word,—*the determination to find fault,*—and fo hard they bear upon the Poet, that I think he would not have oppreffed a Cotemporary with them: particularly if the Author had been a young one, only then rifing to notice. For, inurbane and harfh as Dr. Johnson outwardly appeared, he had great goodnefs of heart, and would not have exercifed fuch undue feverity as might have affected a Writer's fortune, as well as fame. Whereas, by publifhing his Remarks after Pope's demife, he has done *him* lefs injury, and as much fervice to the caufe of Literature. By quickening the Reader's intellect, and enlarging his underftanding, the Critic has freed him from that fuperftitious awe with which he was wont to contemplate the Poet's fhrine.

b   By

By exculpating Johnson from the cruelty of criti᠊
cifm, inafmuch as thofe fevere remarks were not publifhed till after Pope's demife, I do not mean to im᠊
ply that they who adopt the contrary mode of pro-
ceeding are culpable. For that would be to involve
in guilt a very numerous clafs of Critics, indeed,—
the Periodical Reviewers;—whofe exprefs purport
is to pafs judgement on the living. Nor could they
otherwife be of half the fervice to Literature. For in
the *influenza* which at prefent rages—' *Venienti oc-
currite morbo*'—is an aphorifm to be kept in mind:
the *Cacoethes fcribendi*, attacked in time, faves many
an Authorling, whofe difeafe would otherwife foon
become incurable.

But,—granting the fervice which the Critics do to
the commonwealth of Letters, by conducting to the
Temple of Fame thofe who have merit, and excluding
thofe who have none;—do they not fometimes betray
a haughtinefs and contempt bordering upon infolence
towards the rejected Candidates? Do they not fometimes thruft back with a rudenefs ill becoming the
character they fhould maintain, thofe who prefent
themfelves? I have heard fome of them compared to
' Saucy Jacks in office' fond of fhowing their autho᠊
rity, and delighting in laying about their cudgels.

Their Strictures, certainly, are very fevere at times:

more

more or lefs fo according to the difpofition of the perfon brandifhing the pen. Not that I believe their
apparent cruelty often proceeds from malignance, but
moft commonly from an inconfiderate levity of heart,
and the uncontroulable wantonnefs of wit: which
may happily ferve in fome fort as excufe to themfelves,
but is no alleviation of pain to the poor Sufferers.
They, like the pelted Frogs in the Fable, may cry
out,—" Alafs! What is fport to you,—is death to
" us."

It is probable that what I have fpoken thus unre-
fervedly of the wrongheaded or wronghearted Men
amongft the REVIEWERS,—(and what large Society
hath not men of both defcriptions amgonft them?)—
will give thofe very Members offence: but that is
matter of little concern to me; confident as I am that
nothing I have faid can be conftrued into difrefpect for
the REVIEWERS in general, or flight for their works.
To contemn the folly of fome, and reprobate the
malignancy of others, is not to impeach a whole
Clafs;—not, though fpoken of men of ordinary rank:
how much lefs, then, fhall partial cenfure affect the
whole of a learned Society: the majority of whom
muft, neceffarily, from having had a liberal education,
have elevated minds.

In

In FRANCE, where one in every hundred—(which is about the proportion of thofe who can write)—is an Author; and the other ninety nine—(who can hardly read)—are Critics: and where almoft every Province holds its diftinct petty Court of Inquifition upon Authors, I wonder not that the word *Journaliſt* is a term of ignorance and reproach.

But, in GERMANY, and with us, the *Reviewers* furely ftand upon a refpectable footing; and were it not that I know the *Genus irritabile Vatum*, (that Scribblers are not Stoics, but will cry out when they are lafhed)—I fhould be furprifed at the invidious farcafms, and invectives fo frequently and fo unde-fervedly thrown out againft them.

This, if I know my own independency of fpirit, I fay not to curry future favour; nor with reference to their reports of my paft Publications. It is what I faid long before I had any thoughts of ap-pearing in Print. Nor do I fay it in refpect to any particular Perfon; for I have not perfonal acquaint-ance with, nor I do know even by name any one Public Critic in the whole circle of Letters: but I know of what effential ufe their labours are to Literature:—that but for them the World would long ago have been overrun with nonfenfe.

I

I am afraid, SIR, I have almoſt tired you with dwelling ſo long on the ſubject of Criticiſm and Critics. Had it been addreſſed to you only, you might very well twit me with the cant phraſe,—" *Sus Miner-vam* ;"—but, as the *King's Speech* is, by cuſtom of Parliament, debated as the Words of the *Miniſter*, ſo prefatory Diſcourſes, though they have ſome great *Name* or other tacked to them, are looked upon as vehicles of information to *Readers in general.* It was for their ſakes I have endeavoured to ſhow the RE-VIEWERS in a juſt light. For, all the Portraitures I have yet ſeen of them have been taken by partial hands. By theſe they have been repreſented as Giants; by thoſe as dwarfs. By ſome they have been idolized as Demi-gods; and execrated as Devils by others. The extremes are evidently faulty. The truth of every character muſt be taken at the medium, betwixt the partiality of Friends, and the diſlike of Enemies. The Critics certainly make no pretence to ſupernatural powers : nor are they exempted from human frailties. They are Men, like as we (Scribblers) are, variouſly endowed with the qualities of the head and heart.

But now, SIR, it is high time I ſhould ſay ſome-thing of the nature of the Work I have the honour of preſenting to you. And, in ſo doing, I will endea-vour

vour to take the middle courfe, betwixt felf-praife, and felf-condemnation. It is the track we fhould all keep; but it requires more courage, and lefs vanity than generally falls to an Author's fhare.

—— *Juffa monent Heleni Scyllam atque Charibdim*
Inter utramque viam, lethi difcrimine parvo,
Ni teneant curfus.

From whence the proverb,—' *Incidit in Scyllam,* &c.—which I hope will not be verified in me. In fpeaking of this work, I truft I fhall neither be dafhed againft the rock of prefumption, nor drawn into the gulph of defpondency. My little Bark, furely, will get fafe through the Strait, let what may happen to it in the wide Ocean.

I have added to the Title of ' FABLES,'—' AFTER THE MANNER OF LAFONTAINE,'—not to provoke a comparifon of this my Work with that great Mafter's, but merely to diftinguifh it from any thing we have of the Fable kind in our language: unlefs fome forry Tranflations of fome ill-felected from his Fables are thought worthy of that defcription:—which certainly they are not. Had they, fuch as they are, at all refembled the Original, I would as foon have hung up BABRIAS's Head, as LAFONTAINE's, for my Sign.

To

To the Frenchman's honour, and to the credit of
the Moderns, it muſt be owned 'LAFONTAINE's
Work is incomparably ſuperior to that of any ancient
Fabuliſt's, now extant; not excepting PHÆDRUS
himſelf.

In ſaying this you will not ſuſpeᏨ me of giving
undue preference to modern Writers. Few perſons
hold the Ancients in ſuch high eſtimaꞁation as I do.
My partiality, if I have any, leans towards them.
Nor would I part with the little knowledge I have of
the Claſſics for the wealth of all the World. For this
enthuſiaſm which ſtands me in ſo great ſtead, I am
indebted to your late much honoured Father. I ſhall
ever account as the moſt fortunate circumſtance of my
life the having been put to KINGSTON School, under
the tuition of ſuch a *Cultor Juvenum:* as good a
Maſter,—Father,—Iuſband, as good a Man in all
the relative duties of life as ever adorned humanity:—
a thorough Chriſtian; of exemplary morals ; and of
earneſt, unaffeᏨed piety. Occupied, as much of his
time neceſſarily was, by his temporal avocation, no
one could be more aſſiduous in the holy Miniſtry.
And though he died undignified,—neither Biſhop,
Dean, nor Prebendary, (for he had no *parliamentary
Intereſt,)*—his Learning and his Virtues would have
done the higheſt credit to the higheſt Station in the
. Church,

Church. Nor was he unaffected in his piety alone, but in his general manners; in his whole deportment. He did not even study to do good; it was natural to him; and came from him spontaneously. His heart was as enlarged as his underftanding. Quick in his intellects and feelings; and prompt in charity. How many went daily from his doors calling upon Heaven to blefs him! I believe I fpeak within compafs, when I fay, I have myfelf feen him relieve many, many hundreds: and I never faw him turn away one fingle Creature empty handed. So little had he of worldly policy, and the warinefs of narrow minds, that he would have relieved the greateft villain upon earth had he feen him in diftrefs. The probability of being duped was of no confideration with him, when it was poffible he *might* do good. In his reproofs to known Vagabonds he preferved his temper, and his dignity; but did not facrifice his feelings to the affectation of juftice. He confidered the very worft as his fellow-creatures: he gave them lectures, it is true; but he gave them his good-wifhes alfo: and he gave them *money*;—that unequivocal mark of kindnefs and com-paffion.

Poffeffed as my honoured mafter was of every good quality of the head and heart, I have dwelt particu-larly on his charity, becaufe it is the beft virtue Mankind can boaft.

As

As he was beneficent towards the poor; and kind to ftrangers; fo was he clement and indulgent in his School: inflicting punifhment, of neceffity, at times; but much more frequently remitting it.

But what rendered him particularly amiable, and eftimable, was, a genuine truth and fimplicity of character: which, though he lived to a venerable age, and had had much intercourfe with the world, nothing had been able to corrupt. Though it was impoffible but he muft have been witnefs to fcenes of villainy, he was himfelf fo incapable of committing a bafe action, that he was altogether unfufpicious of harm.

Amongft the qualities it was natural to expect in a Perfon whofe time was devoted to Letters, Mr. WOODESON poffeffed others which are not the characteriftics of a Scholar.—He was perfectly well bred: as much fo as if he had paffed his early years at Court, inftead of at College. Courteous, candid, and affable. Agreeable in his perfon, graceful in addrefs, and pleafing in converfation: adapting himfelf with peculiar felicity to the difpofition and capacity of thofe with whom he converfed. Sprightly and jocofe with the young and gay; fedate and argumentative with the learned, and the old.

Of MR. WOODESON's Erudition I might of my own knowledge fay a great deal, having ftudied under him no lefs than ten years; but inftead of ranging over fo wide a field, and writing (which I could do) a whole volume on the fubject; I will confine it to a fingle Anecdote, which I had from a Cotemporary of Mr. W——'s at OxFORD; and which may ferve to give the Reader a tolerable notion of his Learning.

When he was only a Student he was a marked good Scholar: and wrote Verfes (Greek as well as Latin) with fuch facility, that he never refufed his pen to any body. And, as goodnature is often abufed, it happened frequently to him, that, his fel-low Students came to his Rooms at his breakfaft time, and enticing him with fome interefting theme, ate up his breakfaft, whilft he was writing verfes for them.

I leave to the Reader to imagine what a vaft fuper-ftructure of Learning muft have been raifed on fuch a foundation, by the labour of thirty or forty years; affiduoufly teaching, and expounding the beft Claffic Authors. I have, fince I left School, read moft of the Commentators on moft of the Claffics, with fome attention, but never any with half the fatisfaction, nor from any of them have I got half the information I have from the oral expofitions, the learned, juft and elegant criticifms of the late MR. WOODESON, my ever-to-be-remembered, and ever-refpected Mafter.

By

By this my tribute to the worth of one, whofe memory is almoſt as dear to me as it can be to you, I
may, not improbably, have renewed your forrow for
the lofs of fuch a Parent; I may have torn open
thofe wounds which the lenient hand of time had
healed, and have made them bleed afreſh;—yet, SIR,
am I not difpofed to entreat your pardon:—for the
fame reafon that I fhall make no apology to the Reader
for this long Digreffion:—becaufe, it is impoffible to
think of a good Man's removal from Earth to Heaven,
without being better for the reflection.

At the beginning of this Dedication, I intimated
that I had fome fort of excufe to offer for prefuming
to *imitate* LAFONTAINE. The truth is, I was pro-
voked to attempt it by the arrogancy of a Frenchman,
who, not fatisfied with my frank acknowledgement
that we had no Fabuliſt worthy to be compared with
LAFONTAINE, would have it, ' that his Stile was ini-
' mitable; and his Wit of a brilliancy peculiar to the
' Genius of France: and which together would for
' ever mock the efforts of all other Nations, and more
' particularly the *phlegmatic Englifh*.' The impetuous
anfwer I made, I am willing to forget: but the provocation lives in my memory; and thefe Fables are
the fruits of it. Forced fruits have not always the beſt
flavour;

flavour: and so I fear it will be found in this instance: partly, indeed, from my own fault: I was in too great haste to produce them: making the fire in the stoves too ardent; and neglecting from time to time to prune the tree.

As it has been invariably my custom to carry a Book in my pocket: in order to perfect myself in French, when I went abroad, I gave up my Elzivir Classics, (not without great reluctance,) to make room for French Literature; and having met with Lafontaine's Works, amongst others of commodious size, he was on that account, as well as his great merit, commonly my *Compagnon de Voyage*; and almost constantly from the time I purposed to take his likeness. How often have I read him over,—and always with new delight! How often has he regaled my mind,—and my body, too, (by that inexplicable sympathy betwixt our corporal and mental faculties,)— when I have been labouring up the Jura Mountains, in a sultry day! How often have I rambled about the Country of the Lac de Joux, (that delicious Summer Residence,) with nobody to converse with but Lafontaine! And how often, earnestly engaged with him, have I lost my way; and after some pains to find a beaten track, have set me down with Lafontaine, waiting patiently till some chance Traveller,

or

or Peafant came acrofs to direct me home! One
wretched night which I paffed in a Wood, for want
of fuch fortunate occurrence, was made more wretched,
as I thought, than fleeplefs hunger could have made
it, had I but had a light, and LAFONTAINE to have
cheered me. Though, to tell the truth, I was under
fuch apprehenfions of the Aborigines of that Country,—
the Wolves,—that I wifhed more for light by which
to efcape, than to ftudy. What gave full force to my
terrors, was, that I knew for certain a Wolf had paid
a vifit a very little while before, and in the day time
too, at a Village thereabout, and made bold with the
haunch of a Peafant fleeping in a Barn. * Nor
Wolves only, but Bears, wild Boars, and wild Beafts
of all kinds crouded upon my imagination; and I
was ready to cry out with the Epicurift,

———— *Genus horriferum Natura ferarum,*
Humanæ genti infeſtum, terraque marique,
Cur alit?

Happily I efcaped, without other harm than a cold;
but I took care that my favourite Companion fhould
never lead me into fuch another fcrape.

* Such accidents are very rare in Summer time: the Wolves inha-
bit the inacceffible fummits of the JURA, and feldom defcend unlefs
driven by extreme hunger; or diflodged by fnow. The one which
had lately come down was fuppofed to be a female that had loft its
Cub.

To

To get thorough infight into LAFONTAINE, and to acquire his *manner*, I not only read him again, and again; but I tranflated fome of his Fables almoft literally into profe. That tafk, however, I foon gave up; not only from the impoffibility of transfufing the fpirit of one language into another, but that MINERVA has given me too much,—or too little—genius, for fuch employ. Certainly I have not the patience and perfeverance neceffary—*Verbum verbo reddere.* Inftead of which I undertook a very free tranflation in verfe: changing the thoughts, and paraphrafing the wit: till I thought myfelf tolerably adept in his art. Then I ventured to dig for myfelf into the precious mines of ESOP, APTHONIUS, PHÆDRUS, and others. Though I muft own, there are alfo in this collection ten or twelve of bafer metal; a factitious compofition of my own, ftill ftamped after LAFONTAINE's manner. Which thofe particular Fables are it can fcarcely be expected of me to point out: any more than it could be required of a Jew Fabricator, or an Italian Vender of *modern-Antiques* to declare which of his Articles were counterfeits. It is being tolerably honeft, as the World goes, to apprize the Reader that there are two forts. Befide, would it not be paying him too bad a compliment, and myfelf too good a one, to

fup-

fuppofe he could not diftinguifh them, without any
indication from me ?

A Swifs Friend of mine, whofe Vineyards were at
LA COTE, piqued himfelf upon growing excellent
Wine; but, aware of People's prejudice in favour of
what is rare, and foreign, he ufed to tell his Guefts,—
' Meffieurs, there is *Old-Hock*, as well as *Cote* Wine
' upon the table; though the Bottles are only labelled
' No. 1 and 2. Pleafe to tafte of both, and ftick to
' whichever you prefer.'

In fuch fort would I addrefs my Readers. " Mef-
" dames and Meffieurs, I have fet variety of Fables
" before you. Examine them all well: and thofe
" which you like beft, commend the moft: without
" regard to the Inventor;—whether ESOP, PHÆ-
" DRUS, LAFONTAINE, or—Your humble Servant."

But, a further reafon for my not diftinguifhing the
Fables of my *own invention* from the others, was,
that it might look like putting in a claim to thofe
only; whereas I prefume to call the reft my own.
For, excepting two or three very fhort ones, told fim-
ply, and without embellifhment; and about as many
copied from LAFONTAINE, I challenge the whole as
my property.

My claim may, very likely, be called in queftion :
and

and I fhall be told, I have no more right to the *al-tered* Fables, than a Thief has to the Horfes he has ftolen, becaufe, forfooth, he has contrived to difguife them by altering their marks.

The Cafes, I truft, are not exactly parallel. I do not like to be called a Thief, in jeft: not even a lite-rary one; a Plagiary. I have fpread my Toils, 'tis true: and caught a many animals.—But are not Lions, Wolves, and fuch like *feræ naturæ?* Granted, that many of them have PHÆDRUS's, or LA-FONTAINE's marks upon them, having been in their Menageries; can either of them prove any better title than temporary poffeffion? To go back to Esop himfelf, whom we call the *Father of Fable*;—upon what ground do we call him fo? Upon none; but on conjecture. Is there any Manufcript of Esop's extant? Have we any good teftimony that he ever *wrote* a fingle Fable? That he was a witty Fellow the whole World agrees. And fo was LORD CHESTERFIELD; and QUIN; and JOE MILLER eke: but I queftion if they were the Authors of a tithe of the notable fay-ings, which go under their names refpectively. Ne-verthelefs, it may happen in the courfe of a thoufand years, that fome interefted Compiler will collect them all, and what more he can gather, into one vaft vo-lume, and afcribe them to KILLIGREW, or fome

other

other notorious Jefter. And of this we are fure, the anachronic blunders can not be more glaring than thofe in many Fables falfely afcribed to Esop.

I do not mean to revive Difputes which hitherto have tended to no other purpofe than to fhow the acrimony of Men *even of Letters*,—but, I would weaken the force of the objection that may be made to my Book, *for not being entirely original.*

Though my vanity is fo great, that I think I have acquired fomething of LAFONTAINE's Manner; imagine not, SIR, that I pretend to have attained his Excellence. Not that I think *that* fo abfolutely unattainable, as fome have thought.————but, let me not fay any thing to leffen him in the opinion of the World: no: that would look like Envy; a paffion which did not actuate me, when I undertook this Work. (*Non hæc* INVIDIA, *verum eft* ÆMULATIO.) If ever I be bafe enough to injure the fame of true genius; may the Waters of Hippocrene be poifon to me. As long as French Literature lafts LAFONTAINE muft fhine with great refplendence. But, as he fhines in another Hemifphere;—as FRANCE is the meridian of his glory; the only benefit we can receive muft be from the reflection of his rays. And, until a fitter Planet be formed, I would fain ferve as the ufeful Body to reflect his light. And if thought well of by the In-

d   habitants

habitants of Britain, I fhall account my ftation very honourable.

VIRGIL himfelf, *(Divinum illud Latinæ Poëfeos lumen,)* borrowed his light from THEOCRITUS, HE-SIOD, and HOMER; as TERENCE did his from ME-NANDER. HORACE (though in a lefs degree) was beholden to PINDAR; and PHÆDRUS altogether to ESOP. The Fables in the *Greek,* are Diamonds in the rough; in the *Latin,* they are cut and polifhed.

ÆSOPUS auctor quam materiam repperit,
Hanc Ego polivi verfibus fenariis.

ESOP was a Philofopher; and PHÆDRUS was a Poet. But they were both Slaves. LAFONTAINE was well born; and well educated; and was his own Mafter: (as much fo as any Subject can be in FRANCE:) he was tolerably eafy in his circumftances: until inatten-tion to his affairs—(the too common reproach of ge-nius)—made him otherwife. A Penfion, however, and the Patronage of thofe amongft the Great of kin-dred fouls, enabled him to live as much in the *Beau Monde* as was agreeable to a Man of Letters, naturally referved, and taciturne: for, except with felect friends, he fpoke little. In large and mixed Companies, he was filent; making obfervations and reflections; to enable himfelf to fpeak well afterwards—*on paper.*

Such were the advantages LAFONTAINE poffeffed. And

And his Fables, the pleasanteſt Satires that ever were penned, have been the adequate reſult.

When LAFONTAINE is the theme I know not how to leave off. And yet, the more I ſpeak of his Book, the leſs I am inclined to mention my own : which muſt be done, however, ſooner or later.

Having ſo very recently, and ſo highly extolled his Satire, what ſhall I ſay of mine ?—That if it is not quite ſo ſtrong, it is not without force ?—And of my Wit, that if it is not quite ſo keen, it is not altogether without edge? In truth, I have not been ſo ambitious to ſhine, as anxious to pleaſe. But, my chief ſtudy has been to be *uſeful*. For, (as PHÆDRUS well obſerves,)— *Niſi utile eſt quod facimus, ſtulta eſt Gloria.*—" Unleſs our labours have a uſeful tendency, Applauſe is emptineſs."

A ſentiment ſo juſt ought to be engraven, by way of motto, upon every Author's inkſtand. For his own ſake, as well as for the Public's. The *Talents* ſpoken of in the Parable refer in particular to the *Faculties of the Mind*; for the miſapplication of which ' unprofitable Servants will be caſt into outer darkneſs.'

Happily for the World it grows refined in theory, however groſs it may be in practice. Which, though a ſeeming paradox, is certainly true. For, to the ho-

nour

nour of the age be it fpoken, if we except—' The
Trials for adultery,' which ought not to be publifhed,
and ' A Magazine or two,' which ought to be fup-
preffed,—Literature is tolerably chafte. The obfcene
Productions, which fo delighted our Anceftors, would
not only be hiffed off the ftage now, but they would
not be admitted into the Clofets of any, fave old hack-
neyed Lechers, and thoughtlefs, diffolute Apprentices.

Since, then, the *Men* are fomewhat fcrupulous in
their lecture, to whom, or to what fhall we afcribe
the general depravednefs of Morals?—To the im-
proper lecture of the *Women?*—To the pernicious influence of *NOVELS?*—Verily, I believe we may.
Novel-reading, I take to be the fource from whence
corruption flows. Excepting the admirable *Novels* of
RICHARDSON, FIELDING, GOLDSMITH, SMOLLET,
BROOKF, BURNEY, and a few others, every thing
which goes under that title ought to be burned by the
Common Hangman.

If *Books of Chivalry* could be fuppofed to derange
the intellects of fuch a Man as QUIXOTE is defcribed
to be; how fhould *Women-Girls* in the heigh-day of
their blood, when their reafon is as feeble, as their
paffions are ftrong, how fhould they keep their fenfes;
when no other Books are put into their hands, but
Novels; which are exprefsly calculated to make young
folks

folks run riot. In *NOVELS only* Sin is made amiable, and depicted beautiful. There is not a Vice so odious but is therein palliated, or excused; and, not seldom, commended: no Crime so great but is therein authorized by a new Code, called "" SENTIMENT."" A word derived from *sentir*, to feel; and is happily expressive of the fundamental principle of *Novelism*; which is, that every one should act from his own immediate feeling,—from his own whim, and fancy,—from the impressions of the moment; without regard to the established forms of decency, morality, and religion. In short, the doctrine of *Novelism* tends so immediately to debauch the mind, and, in due course, the body,—that I would as soon, a Son of mine should marry a Woman out of a Brothel, as one whose constant lecture has been *NOVELS*.

On this subject I have written more at large in a Work which may one day appear. At present, having deplored the pernicious effects of *Novel-reading*, I have only to add, that, as I fear there is no antidote to this poison when once received into the mind,— no remedy for the Person infected with this pestilence, so is there but one possible way of preventing the contagion spreading: and that is by the *Reviewers* continuing to watch over this, as well as the other departments of literature; sounding the alarm, from time

to

to time : and noticing particularly the Houfes of the Bookfellers, and the Garrets of the Authors where the Plague rages with the greateft violence.

The Reviewers are to be pitied, in that they are conftrained, as literary Phyficians, to vifit fuch infectious Quarters, and have to touch petechial bodies ; neverthelefs, we are fure, they will not fhrink from their duty. It remains, then, with the Keepers of Circulating Libraries, and the Mafters and Miftreffes of Families to take care, not to give admiffion to any *Novels* but thofe which have a certificate of health, figned by the Reviewers.

As *Utility*, that is, the Improvement of Mankind, was the objeft I had chiefly in view in confirufting thefe Fables, I took efpecial care to found them on the folid ground of Religion. Although I was obliged, in conformity to the genius of Fable, to make ufe of the names and charafters of the ethnic Mythology, the doftrines I have inculcated are thofe of Chriftianity.

My *political* Creed is fuch as every thinking Reader muft fubfcribe to ; for it is formed on the Principles laid down by your Predeceffor BLACKSTONE, in his " *Commentaries on the Laws of England* ;" and by YOURSELF, in the " *Elements of Jurifprudence.*" At

one

one and the fame time am I a ftrenuous Affertor of civil
Liberty, and ready to take up arms, (if occafion were)
againft the *Encroachments* of SOVEREIGN POWER,—
but,—whilft the KING confines himfelf within the li-
mits prefcribed by the Conftitution, he has not a more
dutiful or allegiant fubject than I am : nor any one
who would fooner arm in *his* defence.

As far as *Variety* goes towards keeping up the attention, I may venture to affure the Reader, he will not
yawn over this Work: for, befides the common tran-
fition of Fables, from one fubject to another, I
have made ufe of almoft every kind of Metre. By
changing the fabric of my Verfe fo often, certainly
I have confulted the Reader's Liking more than my
own advantage. For, by fo much the more trouble
it gave me, fo much lefs chance I had of attaining to
excellence. It is by uniform practice, and attention to
one fort of ftyle, and one meafure only, that an Author can acquire facility in writing. DR. JOHNSON
has attributed POPE's excellence in verfification to this
very circumftance. And, I hope I may fay it without
offence to MR. HAYLEY, when his Mufe,—who had
a graceful gait of her own,—attempted to, trip it to
ANSTEY's meafure, fhe made a very aukward, and
ungraceful appearance. When BUTLER, who was fo

ex-

excellent in one kind of metre that it has been called, after the name of his Hero, *hudibraftic* verfe,—
when BUTLER quitted that meafure which was fo eafy
and familiar to him, and attempted BOILEAU's, and
other Satires, in decafyllabic verfe, his Pegafus grew
reftif; and refufed to obey the hand of its former
Mafter. So difficult it is, if not impoffible, for thofe
even of the very firft rate abilities to excel more ways
than one.

Why, then, (I fhall be afked) did not I take the
prudent courfe which GAY has taken for his Fables,
and ftand a chance for excellence? Becaufe I defpaired
of attaining to his perfection; and therefore would not
that my Work fhould be put in comparifon with his.—
And, becaufe, I had taken for Exemplar LAFON-
TAINE, whofe varied meafure was better adapted to
my own whimfical and capricious genius.

Thefe Fables will be found to vary as much in
Length as Metre. Some of them are of four or fix lines
only, and others of as many hundred. Thefe latter,
I confefs, are much, very much too long, though I
could name, for precedent, the ingenious MR. MOORE;
whofe whole volume confifts of only fixteen Fables.

It has been a queftion with Commentators,—
' Whe-

Whether the *Moral* fhould ftand at the beginning,
or at the end of the Fable?'—I make no fcruple in
anfwering,—Neither at one, nor the other, *invariably.*—But commonly at the end. For the Reflection grows more naturally out of the Fable, than the
Fable out of the Reflection.

There is no neceffity, however, for the Moral's
ftanding either at the beginning, or at the end; or
apart from the Fable;—but as part of it. Oft times
the Leffon is inculcated to greateft advantage in the
Middle: or, is fo intimately blended with the Story itfelf,
as to require neither diftinct place, nor characters of di-
ftinction. And at fuch times, when one Moral is obvious to every Reader as he runs along; another, a partial
one, may be afterwards pointed out, by the Author.

The Greek Fabulifts, indeed, (or their *officious
Editors,*) have tacked an Επιμυθιον at the end of every
Fable. But, fo difguftingly dry, flat, and infipid are
their reflections, that they are fit only for mere
Children. The Latin ones are not quite fo dull:
but I muft fay, even PHÆDRUS himfelf is too formal
and pedantic a Preceptor.

LAFONTAINE, with the advantage of being born
in later, and more enlightened times, and under ci-
vilized manners, has reaped all the benefit to be expected therefrom. He has appropriated no particular
place to Precepts, and to Gravity. Under the names

and forms of Animals, he has deſcribed the modes of human life. His are not mere *Stories of Cocks and Bulls :* he turns Mens thoughts upon themſelves : laughing at the foibles, and laſhing the vices of Mankind. His *Fables* expoſe to us our Faults, and his *Morals* teach us to amend them.

Such, SIR, are the impreſſions I have received from the lecture of ancient and modern Fables. How far theſe of mine are conformable thereto,—I leave to You and the Public to decide. And for this, amongſt other reaſons, I publiſh a Volume only at a time; that, receiving the benefit of correction, I may ſend ſucceeding ones into the World with fewer imperfections.

Not that I pledge myſelf to follow this up immediately with more Fables, although I have ſo many by me. *Ne quid nimis,* is the motto of the Muſe my Patroneſs : who is not, like THALIA, always on a titter ; nor ever whimpering, like MELPOMENE : but, whimſical, verſatile, various : never two days together in the ſame humour ; and not often two hours :

Sed modo læta manet ; vultus modo ſumit acerbos :
Et tantum conſtans in levitate ſua eſt.

By this deſcription you will take her, poſſibly, to be a terreſtrial Goddeſs ; a fine Lady of this World.— No, Sir. *Ni me ludit amabilis inſania,* She is not only of the divine Siſterhood, Ολυμπια δωματ' εχεσαι,— but the Lady Abbeſs herſelf ; CALLIOPE, *Regina ;*

fkillful

skillful on all inftruments. And I, her Votary, a thrummer upon many. As the Reader may find fome day, to his *coft* ; if I fhould be at the pains of collecting my fcattered Leaves. Out of prudence, perhaps, I had better let them remain difperfed ; as the Sibyl, out of indolence, left hers.

Nec revocare fitus, aut jungere carmina curat.

In this, SIR, I fhould be moft happy to have your judgement to direct me. At all times, and under all circumftances, your criticifms would be invaluable: but more particularly now ; fituated as I am ; a Sojourner in a ftrange Province. The only Perfon hereabout of fuperior abilities, with whom I am at all intimate, has fo little predilection for Poetry, that he is not acquainted even with the Works of the great HAYLEY. To have fhown him my Fables in Manu-fcript, by way of *amufing* him, would have been to prove myfelf in reality as vain, as in burlefque fometimes I would appear. To have read them to him for my own fake, claiming his criticifms as I went along, would have been to impofe upon him a difagreeable tafk, which our acquaintance was not of long ftanding enough to warrant. Whereas I might without fcruple tax a friendfhip of fuch very old date as yours. When you can allow yourfelf relaxation from your feverer ftudies, this Book will be much honoured by your regard. And let me beg of you to favour me with your free and full remarks upon it. Preffed.

Preffed as the *Public Critics* are with Works of Literature, fome of great merit, and others of import-
ance; this little Volume cannot expect from them
much notice: unlefs, indeed, it be from the CRITICAL
REVIEWERS; who thought both my former Publications worthy of their particular note. Of their Account of the latter I fhall beg leave to extract a Paffage,
not only becaufe I am proud of their general commen-
dation, but am ready to acknowledge the juftice of
their partial cenfure.

" The old Tale of SOCRATES AND XANTIPPE, the *ftormy Tale*
" terminated by the *Shower*, is humoroufly verfified in the little pam-
" phlet now before us. We need not enlarge on the fubject, but
" muft exprefs our approbation of the Author's talents in the burlefque
" ftyle. MR. WALLBECK might have obtained more of our praife,
" if his humorous levity, in one or two paffages, had been better re-
" ftrained; though we fhould add, that we have met with nothing
" very exceptionable. The following advice makes ample amends
" for any tranfitory error."——

(*Then follow the felected Stanzas.*)

The exceptionable words, to which my *Critical Ad-
monifher* alludes, were fuch as firft prefented themfelves
to my indignant mind, but they fhall certainly be al-
tered before the *TALE* goes again to prefs.

To liberal Criticifm I fhall ever pay the greateft deference; as you will find, whenever you favour me
with yours.

I am, SIR,

Your much obliged Friend,

And obedient humble Servant,

THE AUTHOR.

ANCIENT and MODERN:

AFTER THE MANNER OF

L A F O N T A I N E.

F A B L E   I.

E S O P   A T   P L A Y.

A S Esop was with boys at play,
A grave *Athenian* pafs'd that way;
And ftraight began to mock at him:
' Was ever fo abfurd a whim !—
' What will the Academics fay,
' Hearing that Esop ftoops to play
' With Children ?—O, MINERVA ! when
' Will men behave themfelves like men ?'
   Th' apoftrophe made Esop fmile,
Who yet kept playing all the while:

B   ' But,

' But, tell us, (the *Athenian* cries)—
' You who affect to be fo wife,—
' What is your reafon? Doubtlefs, you
' Some reafon have for what you do.'

' *See you that unftrung Bow that lays*
' *Befide you?*'—ESOP quaintly fays.
' I fee it plain enough: what then?'

' *But look at it, grave Sir, again.*'
' Pfhaw!—this is childifhnefs: I fee
' The Bow:—what anfwer is't to me?'
ESOP at his impatience fmiled:
' *Which of us, think you, is the child?*
' *Or,—fhall I out with it at once,—*
' *Which of us, think you, is the dunce?*

' *Can any thing in nature fhow*
' *My meaning better than that Bow?*
' *Were't always ftrung, for ever bent,*
' *Its force elaftic would be fpent.*
' *But being, when unufed, left loofe,*
' *'Tis ftronger, fitter far for ufe.*

' *'Tis fo exactly with the human mind:*
' *Who keeps it on the ftretch for aye, will find*
' *Its ftrength impair'd; and, when too late, repent*
' *It was not now and then with* play *unbent.*'

F A B L E

F A B L E   II.

THE TWO CRABS.

A CRAB at bottom of the ocean
  Was heard her daughter to deride;
' Arrah, my Dear; keep ftill that motion:
' And don't walk forward all a-fide.'

Young CRAB replies,—' Is't not a fhame—
' *You* of all folks fhould keep this bother?
' Pray, which of us is more to blame?
' *Who fet th' example?*—I, or mother?'

So plain this Fable's moral is,
It cannot conftrued be amifs.
Exact not of your child what you
Find it impoffible to do.

Bother,] This word in common ufe with the Irifh, has a fignification almoft fimilar to our *pother*; but of greater ftrength, and energy.

F A B L E   III.

The GRASSHOPPER and the ANT.

A GRASSHOPPER, who blithe and gay
Had danced the Summer months away,
Forgetting Winter was to come,
Laid no provision in at home:
Nor wheat, nor rye, or good or bad;—
No stock of any kind he had.

Shivering with cold, and pinch'd with want,
He hies him to the thriftier ANT;
‘ Dear Creature, be so kind (says he)
‘ To lend me from your granary
‘ Some twenty thousand grains of wheat,—
‘ Barley, or any thing to eat.
‘ In Autumn next I'll pay the whole,
‘ With thanks:—I will, upon my soul.’

‘ I cannot say,——(replies the ANT)
‘ Last harvest was so very scant,——
‘ Whether I any have to spare.
‘ But, prithee, tell me first, where are
‘ Your pledges;——your security?’

‘ What,

'What is't you mean ;—to talk to me
' Of pledges, and fecurity?—
' Good Mafter Cit, that's too abfurd :
' Is't not enough I pledge my word?
' We GRASSHOPPERS are Gentlemen,—
' Although we borrow now and then.'

'*From me far be it to difpute*
'*The word of fuch a well-born brute.*
'*An humble Citizen to fcan*
'*The conduct of a Gentleman!—*
'*O fie.—But, if without offence,*
'*I might, in name of Common Senfe,*
'*Demand, great Sir, what have you done*
'*With all your wealth? Or, had you none?*
'*If of your own no flocks, nor lands*
'*You had, why not employ your hands,*
'*Or head, in Summer, to contrive*
'*How in the Winter you might live?*'

' That's true, (the GRASSHOPPER replies ;)
' I fhould have done't, had I been wife.
' Inftead of which, the Summer through,
' Pleafure alone I had in view :
' Frequented all the public places ;
' Drefs'd in embroidery, and laces ;
' And ftudied nothing but the graces :
' Talk'd with the Lords ; danced with the Ladies,—
' Once with a Dutchefs ;—*who afraid is?*'

'*I wifh*

' *I wish you joy, with all my heart.*
' *Good morning, Sir:—you may depart.*
' *Your fortune must be far advanced*
' *With those fair Dames with whom you danced,*

' *Call at their doors; it were a sin,*
' *Should they refuse to let you in.*
' *What! Such a sprightly Spark as you,*
' *That caper'd all the Summer through!*
' *I'll lay my life on't, you can sing,*
' *Cold as the weather is, till Spring.*
" *To dance and sing"—'s a pretty trade:—*
' *Go to the Ladies;——who's afraid.*'

FABLE

F A B L E IV.

The OLD MAN and DEATH.

AN aged HIND returning from the wood
With faggots on his back, too great a load,
He let them fall, and, with the world at ſtrife,
Began in petulance on DEATH to call :—
' Ah ! Would that DEATH, he who alleviates all,
' Would come, and put a period to my life !'

The hideous SKELETON before him ſtands,
As ſoon as call'd; and aſks him—' *His commands?'*—
(Shaking his dart) " *Now—ſhall I end your pain?*"—
The OLD MAN frighten'd turns his face away;
And ſcarce, with fault'ring accent can he ſay,—
' My faggots have fall'n off; pray lift them on again.'

———— ———— Who would fardles bear
And groan and ſweat under a weary life,
But that the dread of ſomething after death,—
(That undiſcover'd country, from whoſe bourne
No Travèller returns,)—puzzles the will ;
And makes us rather bear thoſe ills we have,
Than fly to others that we know not of ?
SHAKSPERE.

This admirable Reflexion of our immortal Bard's is ſo appoſite to
the FABLE, that I have no doubt he had it in his *mind's eye*, when
he penned that part of HAMLET's Soliloquy. For having inſerted
it in the ſtead of any Moral I could have drawn, no Reader of ſenſe
will find fault with me : and as to others,—who have no reliſh
but for novelty ; and who prefer every thing that is *new*, *becauſe*
it is new ;—I exclude them all together from the Temple of Taſte.
Εκας, εκας ιοῖς βεϐηλοι.

FABLE

F A B L E V.

The BOY ASLEEP and FORTUNE.

A Thoughtlefs SCHOOLBOY, tired with play,
   Was fleeping by a river's fide:
FORTUNE, who chanced to pafs that way,
Waked him, and thus began to chide:

' Was ever little Urchin found
   ' In greater peril! Up, for fhame:
' Had *you*, by your own fault, been drown'd,
   ' *I* had unjuftly born the blame.'

'TIS the fame ftory with us all:
Whatever foolifh things we do;—
Whatever fcrapes we get into;—
Dame FORTUNE *to account we call.*

FABLE

F A B L E   VI.

The TWO CATS and the MONKEY.

A T Midnight, when the Novice fleeps,
The lufty Friar from his cell
To the expecting Abbefs creeps.
How they keep vigil,—need I tell?

Prowlers of every kind and fort,
At dark, their hiding-places leave;
Some bent on mifchief; fome on fport:
Thefe to take pleafure, thofe to thieve.

ONE night, whilft Goodman PLOUGHSHARE flept,
Two CATS into his larder crept,
Through broken pane; and ate their fill;
And carried prog away at will:
Small articles: but left behind
The larger;—much againft their mind.
Some beef in falt; and flitch of bacon;
Good of their kind: or I'm miftaken.
But nothing feem'd fo well to pleafe
Their nerves olfact'ry as a Cheefe:

C   A

A STILTON one:—and I defy
All PARMA; and all ITALY;
And SCHOPZEGA; and GRUYIERES;—
(More famed for Cheefes now, than Bears,)
To make a better. 'T was fo good,
Our CATS, who Eating underftood,
Declared, in all their lives that they
Ne'er took fo good a one away.
They roll'd it round and round, and fain
Would pafs it through the broken pane:
They tried their utmoft—but in vain.

    The difappointment much provoked
Their Catfhips; they their whifkers ftroked,
Indignantly; their teeth they gnafh'd;
And fwollen tails with fury lafh'd.

    GRIMALKIN imprecations mumbled
In a low mewl; and growl'd, and grumbled:
But t'other, TABBY Reprobate,
In louder accents curs'd his fate.
" May furies,—demons,—mad dogs tear—
('Tis no new thing for Cats to fwear)
" My vitals,—as I do this hair.—"
He ftopp'd; and from his brindled cheft
Tore hair enough to've made a neft,
(Inftead of male if he had been
A female,)—to have kitten'd in.

                  " Curft

" Curft fortune !—Shall we all night toil
" For nothing ! Labour fo, and moil,
" Torment us, tantalize and teafe,
" With the vain hope of fuch a cheefe !

" If we can't compafs it ere day,
" May LETHUM take my lives away;—
" All nine of 'em ! My death is built on
" The difappointment of this Stilton."

' Hold ! impious Epicure;—(replies
' GRIMALKIN ;)—" vent not blafphemies.
' I've hit upon a way, I trow,
' To do it.'—" Have you ? *Quomodo ?*"—
' Obferve. I'll do it by myfelf.'—
He faid; and roll'd it off the fhelf.
Expedient fortunate: for, lo !
The Cheefe, by falling, broke in two.
And, what, when whole it could not do,—
The window pafs,—at twice went through.

Superlative felicity !
What happier Cats on earth could be ?
None, you would think.—O ! fad reverfe.
Thieving's attended with this curfe;
What, at the hazard of their lives,
Rogues get, not only never thrives,
But ev'n in fharing, they fall out,
Nine times in ten, their fpoil about.

The

The piece of Cheese, which 'twixt her paws
GRIMALKIN held, the larger was;
A very little; but enough
To put young TABBY in a huff.
From him, the moſt iraſcible
Of Cats, theſe ireful accents fell.
" Think not, ſo cunning as you are,
" To carry off that larger ſhare.

" I've often heard, and find it true,
" GRIMALKIN, there's no truſting you.
" You bring up thieves; and cheat 'em too.
" But fancy not, I am ſo young
" To let grey whiſkers do me wrong.
" No: you ſhall do me fully right;
" Give me that piece: or forthwith fight."

GRIMALKIN who not fighting loved;
And was not eaſy to be moved;
When he ſaw TABBY's choler riſe,
And lightning flaſhing from his eyes,
Reſolved if poſſible t' appeaſe
His fury, and yet keep the Cheeſe.
' Yes, TAB, you 're young,—and very young,
' To think that I would do you wrong.
' On no account would I offend,
' And much leſs cheat ſo dear a friend.

' If I decline with you to fight
' It is not that I mean to flight
' Your years; be fure, I know your worth;
' There's not a braver Cat on earth.
' But, 'twere a pity fight we fhou'd;
' No;—I'll not fpill fuch precious blood.

    ' As to our fhares, I do not know
' Mine larger is; but be it fo;
' Recall to memory, if you pleafe,
' Which of us firft fmelt out the Cheefe:
' And by whofe artifice and wit,
' We got, and are enjoying it.'

    After much wrangling, noife, and pother;
Splutt'ring, and fpitting at each other,
Till they were weary: they agreed
Straightway to JUSTICE PUG to fpeed,
And before him their caufe to plead.

    The Parties to the JUSTICE come,
Are fhown into his Worfhip's room:
Where in an elbow-chair he fat,
Lolling with magifterial ftate.
' *Well, Sirs, what bufinefs brings you here?*—
' *What are thofe parcels you have there?*'—
"' Shall I not fwear 'em?'"—' *As you pleafe:*
' *And, harkee!—don't forget your fees.*'

The

The Parties fworn; the fhillings paid;
GRIMALKIN waved his paw, and faid:
' May't pleafe your Worfhip, TAB and I
' Agreed a Stilton Cheefe to buy;—
' We bought one: took it home, and tried
',In equal portions to divide
' The fame: and equal fure they are;
' But TAB thinks mine the larger fhare.
' I,—knowing your decifions true,
' Moft willingly appeal to you.'

" An' pleafe your Worfhip, TABBY cries,
" This cream-lapper, with Tiger eyes—*
" But in his heart a very Moufe,
" Would fain me—valorous TABBY,—choufe.
" This coward wretch who dares not fight,
" Would cheat a Hero of his right.

" I come to you, Sir, for redrefs;
" Unwillingly, I muft confefs:
" For, rather I by force of *paw*
" Would battle it,—than force of Law."

PUG puffs his cheeks, and looking big,
Draws forward his enormous wig;

* *This cream-lapper, with Tiger eyes*—&c.
Οινοβαρες, κυνος ομμαῖ εχων, κραδιην δ'ελαφοιο, &c.

Preffing

Preſſing it cloſe : elſe might they ſee
Where his two auricles *ſhould be :*—
For, loug time ſince were both his ears
Cut off, with certain wooden ſhears,
Yclept a Pillory, wherein
For theft, and other *petty* ſin,
Such as falſe-ſwearing, he had been.
Since made a JUSTICE, from belief
No one's ſo fit to catch a thief,
(As the old proverb ſays,) as He
That practiſed is in thievery.
Who elſe ſhould know their haunts ſo well?—
Their various arts, and tricks who tell ?

All Magiſtrates the trade ſhould learn:
Theſe have been Rogues ; and thoſe read BURN.
The worſt are they, who, from a turn
Litigious, get into the *Quorum* ;
And drive their Neighbours all before 'em.
Some for the honour only pant :
And others occupation want.

There are, indeed,—(would more there were !)
Magiſtrates who the office bear
With dignity : on it reflect
A luſtre ; and command reſpect.
Such we our Country's Worthies term :
Who, not officious are, but firm :

Who,

Who, to the Poor impartial law
Deal out ;—and keep the Rich in awe.
Who, nor connexions have, nor friends,
So long as any Suit depends ;
But fit, whoe'er the Parties be,—
In foro CONSCIENTIÆ.
Who, not intimidated are
By Ruffians' threats ; but fearlefs wear
The fword ; and no Delinquents fpare :
For cowardice, or mercy fhown,
Through a falfe tendernefs, to one,
Thoufands and thoufands has undone.
He who the feelings of his heart
Confults, can act no public part.

But, you muft not mifconftrue me
—Into undue feverity.
When the Cafe will of doubt admit,
You muft the Prifoner acquit.
‘ Better that twenty guilty fhou'd
‘ Efcape, than we fhould fhed the blood
‘ Of one man innocent.’ So fays
The Englifh Law, to England's praife.

I would afk pardon of the Reader,
For turning here a Special Pleader ;
But that the Mufe's aberration
Is for the good of all the nation.

Apparent my defign, I truft is,
A wholefome Lecture upon Juftice.
Into COMMISSION I would urge
Wife Men: and Fools, and Scoundrels fcourge.

But,—to my Fable.—PUG, who loved
Good Cheefe, was by the odour moved:
And, coughing confequentially,
Says to the Clerk; ' *Hem!—Let me fee*
' *This Stilton.—*MITTIMUS *!—Where arc*
' *My Scales?—I ought to have a pair.*'

''' You *ought:* (the Clerk farcaftic fays:)
''' There was a pair in DIGNUS' days.
''' But the firft time your Worfhip came
''' You bent, and after broke the beam.''''

' *It is no matter,* PUG *replies*;
' *I have, thank* JOVE, *a pair of eyes*
' *That, without fpectacles, can fee*
' *Which of thefe pieces larger be.*
' *Ay:—this is it:—'tis, therefore, fit*
' *I nibble off a little bit.—*
' *Delicious!—But, I have not ta'en*
' *Off quite enough:—I'll try again.—*
' *Odfo! I've ta'en too much, I trow:—*
' *The other feems the bigger now.*

D

' *The*

' *The only difficulty lies*
' *In bringing t'other to this fize.*
' *I'll do fo.*————*Poh!—How bad a guefs!—*
' *This which too large was, is the lefs.*

' *I'll try again;—I'll fpare no pains,*
' *Whilft any of the Cheefe remains.*
' *To fay the worft of it, 'tis good;*
' *And is, befides, my favourite food.*
' *Happily, too; my appetite*
' *Is keen: I'll have another bite.*'

The CATS at length began to fmoke,
But relifh'd not, the MONKEY's joke:
Their fhares fo rapidly diminifh'd,
Two other bites the whole had finifh'd:
Which made GRIMALKIN thus addrefs,
In hafte, the JUSTICE;—' Sir, you guefs
' So very badly; if you pleafe,
' We will ourfelves divide the Cheefe:—
' I rather fhould have faid—the *Rind*;
' For cheefe it would be hard to find.
' Ah! Would we had been fatisfied;
' And not YOUR WORSHIP to applied!
' If it is thus you juftice do;
' 'Tis the laft time we'll come to you.

' We did not mean to cram your maw
' Voracious;—No:—we wanted *Law.*'

'Ye Oafs! Ye know not what ye want,
'Law!—Is not Law a Cormorant?'—

'It feems fo, Sir:—but pray you fpare
'The reft: the Law has had her fhare.'

'Firft;—have you cafh to pay your fees?
'If not,—the remnant of the Cheefe
'Muft go my Clerk to fatisfy.
'MITTIMUS takes the fees;—not I.'

"E'en take it, then;—and, Sir; if e'er
"We come again to you, to fhare
"Our property,—we'll pay you double,—
"Ay, treble charges, for your trouble.
"We underftand your Law;—we fmoke you:—
"Keep the Cheefe rind, and—
(afide)——"may it choak you."

F A B L E

F A B L E   VII.

The MILLER, *and his* MULE.

WRetched the Land which is War's theatre!
  Nobles and Peasants live in constant fear.'
At the least noise, at every little stir,
They start, and cry—' *The Enemy is near.*'

A MILLER once, alarm'd, urged on his BEAST;
 " Haste! or we shall be ta'en. O, dire disaster!"—
The MULE replies,—' *I'm not in so much haste :—*
' *I cannot be worse off, whoe'er's my Master.*'

·There is one way, and only one, to bind
Dependants :—Be compassionate, and kind.
 When *Subjects* are thought worth their *Prince's* care,
Then will they prove how well attach'd they are.
 O'er BRITAIN ever *should* a Tyrant reign;
And dare attack our Liberties again :
I trust there will be Patriots in the Land
Ready to wrest the Sceptre from his hand.
 But, thanks to Heaven, we've now upon the Throne,
A KING who makes our Interests his own.
Long may he live :—and *HIS SUCCESSOR* prove
Discreet, and worthy of his People's Love.

F A B L E

F A B L E VIII.

The BUTTERFLY and the DOVE.

A BUTTERFLY, though in decline
  Of life, ftill vaunted to a DOVE;
'He was a gallant Libertine.'
  And laugh'd at Conftancy in Love.

'Oh! what a contraft I could draw
  'Betwixt my gay, and your dull life!
'Each pretty BUTTERFLY I faw
  'I kifs'd:—you've only kifs'd your wife.

''Tis true, times are a little changed;
  'When young I had them at my call,
'From one to other freely ranged:—
  'Now they avoid me, one and all.'

'*Yes:—you have much to boaft, in footh!—*
  '*The* DOVE *replies, in fatire bold.*
'*With Harlots you have pafs'd your youth:*
  '*And they difpife you, now you're old.*

'*How*

‘ *How much more happily We live,*
‘ *Whom, as infipid, you defpife :*
‘ *But you miftake ; we* Doves *can give*
‘ *Example to you* Butterflies.

‘ *Inftead of your unhallow'd fires ;*
‘ *Your guilty, tranfitory joy ;*
‘ Hymen *improves our chafte defires :*
‘ *Felicity without alloy.*

‘ *Love which in youth takes kindly root,*
‘ *Does every day more vigorous prove.*
‘ *In age itfelf it yields us fruit :*
‘ *'Tis* FRIENDSHIP *grafted upon* LOVE.’

F A B L E

F A B L E — IX.

The DOG and his SHADOW.

A LURCHER, a notorious thief,
From fhambles ftole a piece of Beef:
To take it home, he needs muft pafs
A Stream: the ftream, as fmooth as glafs,
Prefented feemingly to view
Another Dog; like loaded, too:
Forthwith a plunge the LURCHER made,
In greedy hope to fpoil the SHADE:
And as he open'd wide his chops
To do fo, down his own piece drops.

This *doggifh* Character is meant
For every one, who, not content
With his poffeffions, cafts an eye
Towards his neighbour's property.

To thofe whom jeeringly we call
NABOBS—what ufe their ill-got fpoil?

Loaded

Loaded with *Wealth* if they return
From INDIA, they for *Honours* burn.
That, which they might enjoy, they lofe
By the extenfion of their views.
Nobles in fplendour they outvie :
Build Palaces ; and Boroughs buy ;—
Till brought again to poverty.

Much might they with their fortunes do ;
Be liked ;—almoft refpected too.
But, far from being courteous, they
Grow more imperious every day.
So far from ftriving to do good,
They're curfes to their neighbourhood.
And, living to no worthy end,
Die without having made a Friend.

FABLE

FABLE X.

The FOX and the WOLF.

BY fome mifchance poor RENARD fell,
Heels-over-head, into a Well.
At the laft gafp almoft he lay,
When he heard fome one pafs that way:
And juft had ftrength enough to yelp;—
" Help,—charitable Pagan;—help!"

The WOLF look'd down, and though he found
The wretched Creature nearly drown'd,
He leifurely harangued him;—' Pray,
' What were you doing, Sir, this way?
' Oft as I've prowl'd this Country o'er,
' I never met you here before:
' And now in what condition met!
' 'Tis ten to one but you are wet.
' How fell you in?'
                    " Nay, never wafte
" Time in enquiry:—prithee, hafte
" To help me. When I'm *out*,—I'll tell
" By what misfortune *in* I fell."

How People flock about a Stranger
In the Streets dying, or in danger!
'Tis CURIOSITY, *I fear,*
More than COMPASSION, *draws 'em there.*

E   *FABLE*

F A B L E XI.

The FARMER, the FOX, and the DOG.

BEFORE one hires a Houfe, 'tis good
T' enquire about the Neighbourhood.
None but a Thief himfelf would choofe
To live amongft the DUKE's-PLACE JEWS.

I fhould not like to take a Farm
Where Foxes, Wolves, and Vermin fwarm.
Not only 'bout one's grounds they roam,
   By night and day;
   And fure as Kids, or Lambkins ftray,
   Make 'em their prey;—
But vifit even our chicken-coops at home.

NATHLESS, a FARMER (fays the Fable)
   So wary was, a Fox in vain,
Week after week, was ufed to watch
The poultry yard; and was not able
A fingle ftraggling Chick to catch:
He had his ' labour only for his pain.'
    " Safe bind,
    " Safe find."
So fays the proverb; and fo thought our HIND.
                    He

He every night in henhoufe puts
His fowls : and doors and windows fhuts.
RENARD, in hope to find fome place unbarr'd,
Comes every night into the FARMER's yard :
Into each hole, and corner pries,
Not even except the Sties :
For he has no diflike to Pig,
If very nice, and not *too big :*
For the fame reafon too, the Glutton
Loves Lamb, but cannot *manage* Mutton.
Nought comes amifs that's portable : ·
But if his Fox-fhip were to choofe,
With poultry he would deck his table ;
Turkey, or fowl ;—or duck, or goofe.
For this he comes night after night ;
Moon, or no moon ; pitch-dark, or light ;
Sundays,—Saint-days,—and Holidays ;
All times of year ; all nights of week ;
RENARD's no *Jew* ;—(JOSEPHUS fays ;)—
(And let ME add)—no *Catholic.*
If all be faft, he does but ftay
To curfe himfelf ;—that is,—to fay
A pray'r or two—the backward way.

To fay one's prayers the backward way,] Is not to be taken
literally ; as beginning with ' Amen,' and finifhing with the firft
word ; but in its figurative fenfe. When any one, inftead of humbly
acquiefcing in the difpenfations of Providence, calls their fitnefs in
queftion ;—fuch an impious Remonftrance may be termed " Saying
one's prayers the backward way."

' How

' How hard my fate, O, partial Jove !
' Is this your univerfal Love?
' Shall fuch a defpicable race
    ' As Cocks and Hens your favour reap;
' Well fed by day; and have a place
    ' Wherein at night fecure to fleep ?—
' Whilft *I*, of better parts and worth,
    ' Am forced fo many miles to roam
' For food : then, hide me in the earth;
' A cold uncomfortable home.'

Infolent Wretch! To dare profane
The equity of Jove, becaufe
Of other Creatures care was ta'en,
That they not fell beneath his paws.

It happ'd, howe'er, the FARMER having kept
Late market once, came home with wine in's head;
Of fenfe and cuftomary prudence reft,
Leaving his doors unlock'd he went to-bed.

To make my ftory fhort:—The Fox,
Without or forcing bars or locks
The Hen-rooft enter'd : you may guefs,—
(For it would tire the Mufe to tell,)
How many millions, more or lefs,
To glut his maw and fury fell.
Sure fuch a day,—nor night, I ween,
By Sun or Moon was ever feen !—

                                        Unlefs

Unlefs it was when DIOMED
Fell upon RHESUS by furprife;
And cut off many a Thracian's head,
Ere it had time to ope its eyes.
PHOEBUS turn'd pale, as well he might,
At fuch a fanguinary fight.
' Pſhaw! What is PHOEBUS to the tale?—
' How turn'd the FARMER? Was he pale?'

Unlefs it was when DIOMED, *&c.*] This is not the Incident by
which LAFONTAINE chofe, in his burlefque way, to illuftrate the
mighty Slaughter; but I think it more appofite than either of thofe
which he has felected, from HOMER. That the Reader, however,
may judge between us, I will tranfcribe both his paſſages.

> *Tel, et d'un fpectacle pareil*
> APOLLON *irrité contre le fier* ATRIDE,
> *Ioncha ſon champ de morts. On vit prefque détruit*
> L' *oſt des Grecs; et ce fut l'ouvrage d'une nuit.*
> *Tel encore autour de ſa tente*
> AJAX *à l'ame impatiente,*
> *De moutons et de boucs fit un vafte débris,*
> *Croyant tuer en eux ſon concurrent* ULYSSE,
> *Et les auteurs de l'injuftice*
> *Par qui l'autre emporta le prix.*
> Le RENARD, *autre* AJAX, *aux volailles funefte,*
> *Emporte ce qu'il peut, laiſſe étendu le refte.*

Though I flatter myfelf I have been more happy than LAFON-
TAINE in the parrallel I have drawn; I pray the Reader not to mifconftrue me into the prefumption of coping generally with fo great a
Mafter. But,—great Mafter as he is, I fcorn to be his mere Copyift.
No:—though I have on many Subjects taken outlines from him,
and on all profefs myfelf his Imitator, I truft I fhall not be found
fervilely fo. His *ſtile,*—his *manner* is what pleafes me; but I beg
leave to *think* for myfelf.

Patience,

Patience, good Sir; and you ſhall hear.
Soon as he came the Hen-rooſt near,
And found the portal ope, aghaſt he ſtood:
Then, caſting fearfully his eyes around,
Saw walls and perches ſtain'd with chicken blood;
And many a mangled carcaſe ſtrew'd the ground.
Ah, me!—ah *him!* (I mean)—who eyed
The ſcence of carnage; petrified
Almoſt with grief; elſe had he cried.
But, he bethought him ſoon to call
His Servants round, and ſcold them all.
For ſo egregious is Man's pride,
With moſt of us 'tis cuſtomary,
Fall out what will, what will miſcarry,
T' excuſe ourſelves,—blame all the world befide.

Poor TRAY, who chanced to be at hand,
Received the heavieſt reprimand.
' And *you,* you good-for-nothing Dog,
' To lay as ſenſeleſs as a log;
' And not alarm us ! not one yelp!—
' You ſhall be hang'd, you worthleſs Whelp.'

" Sir, (replies TRAY,)—'twould ill become
" Me to put arguments too home:—
" A four-legg'd Brute make an oration
" Againſt a Lord of the Creation !—

" Elſe,—

" Elfe,—I'd one queſtion aſk;—no more.—
" *Who* was't left ope the Henhouſe door?
" Had that been faſt, no thief had ventured
" To touch the latch; much leſs have enter'd.
" I'd have bark'd loud enough to rouſe
" The greateſt *Drunkard* in the Houſe."
TRAY argued well, we muſt allow;—
Too well;—a Tyrant cannot bear
Unpleaſant truths ſhould reach his ear.
So far from willing to avow
His fault; the FARMER ſeized on TRAY,
And hung him up that very day.

———————————

BY way of Epilogue, I'll tell you, Maſters,
What this long Fable meant:
The only method to prevent
Robberies, and other ſuch Diſtaſters,
Is,—' *To get early home; keep cool the head:*
' *Shut all the doors yourſelf: and go the laſt to bed.*'

FABLE

FABLE XII.

The MOUNTAIN in LABOUR.

PARNASSUS in Labour,
   Alarm'd every Neighbour ;
The MUSES, and even APOLLO.*
Well might it aftound
Poor Mortals all round,
   Expecting an Earthquake would follow.

LUCINA in waiting ;
And Goffips a-prating,—
   " Good lack ! what a terrible bout !"
Credibile Dictu ?———
(Dan PHAEDRUS I ftick too ;—)
   A minikin MOUSE tumbled out.

   This Fable regards
   Ourfelves, Brother Bards ;
     When Pegafus fets off too faft.
   Who fpurs at beginning ;—
   May fancy he's winning ;—
     But knocks the old hack up at laft.

---

* *Alarm'd the* MUSES *and* APOLLO.] It has been faid JOVE himfelf was frighted : Ωδινεν ορος. ΖΕΥΣ δ'εφοβειτο :—thinking,
perhaps, the Giants were moving Mountains again. But as Poets
have more to do with PARNASSUS, than with PELION or OSSA,
I have taken the Fable in the fame fenfe HORACE has.

                        FABLE

F A B L E   XIII.

The D o g, and the C r o c o d i l e.

W E Men by reafon, Brutes by inftinct know,
      Into what Company 'tis fafe to go.
Yet,—with our boafted reafon, vaunted fenfe,
How oft do we mifplace our confidence.
To Widows tears we truft, and Harlots fmiles :—
But Dogs are never fond of CROCODILES.

Thefe dreadful Creatures,—(Crocodiles I mean,)—
About the Nile fo frequently are feen,
That Dogs compell'd by thirft extreme to drink,
Not without caution venture to the brink :
Nor at one place dare lap till they have done;
But fhift their ground, ftill lapping as they run.

A CROCODILE addrefs'd a DOG one day :—
‘ Why in fuch hafte ?—I prithee, honeft TRAY,
‘ Let us confabulate a little.————Nay !
‘ Now you 're unfociable.—Why run away ?
‘ If you 'll not talk ; e'en ftop, and drink your fill.

“ Thank you, (fays TRAY ;) another time I will :
“ But in good footh, I am fo very fhy,
“ I cannot drink when CROCODILES are by.”

F   *FABLE*

F A B L E   XIV.

The WOLF'S REMONSTRANCE.

A WOLF pafs'd by a Shepherd's cot,
Juft as a Sheep's-head fmoking hot,
Tongue, Brains, and all, was put on table.
' Ye two-legg'd Animals! (fays he,)
' Is 't fit ye fhould find fault with me,
  ' Who are yourfelves fo culpable?

' When at your Feafts ye dine, or fup,
' Ye eat whole Geefe and Chickens up:
  ' Oft have I caught you in the faɛt.
' Nay;—and I tell you to your face,
' GOODY; I heard you *once* fay grace.—
  ' For fhame!—What,—glory in the aɛt?

' If *I*— a hungry WOLF, alack!—
' Now and then take a little fnack,
  ' Of Kid, or Calf, or Lamb, or Mutton;—
' Some Cur the neighbourhood alarms;
' And ye againft me take up arms,
  ' Becaufe,—forfooth, I am a *Glutton*.'

AS inconfiftent Men tow'rds Men:
Yet juft we think ourfelves, as wife.
Keen enough *others* faults to ken,
Againft our *own* we fhut our eyes.

FABLE

F A B L E XV.

The Rats in Common-Hall.

IN England—much about the time
When Tyranny was in its prime—
But why fhould Englifhmen be pain'd
By recollecting now who reign'd
So long ago? No; let it pafs:
'Tis bootlefs to lament what *was*.
  Befides, the Story tells as well
Of Beasts; and is more laughable.

  IN days of yore, the Rats, a Nation
Of confequence in the Creation,
Inhabiting our Ifle, complain'd
How favage was the Cat that reign'd:
Norman by birth: Grimalkin hight:
Stranger to every foft delight.
The chace was all he underftood,—
And War; and much he joy'd in blood:
So much, that every day he flew
A Subject Rat; and fometimes two.
And not content with murdering, *eat*,
And thought them moft delicious meat.
Lit'rally fo; not, as we fay,
French Slaves are fed on every day.

                                    Louis,

LOUIS, we know, cannot devour
His Subjects, but by metaphor.
No more an *Anthropophagus*
Is He than NORTH, who draws from us
Our deareſt blood :—our caſh, I mean.
His Impoſts make us wond'rous lean ;—
The richeſt of us : but the Poor
No longer can his gripe endure.
Is 't fit they periſh, to ſupport
Him ;—or THE GREATEST MAN at Court?
But—hold thy too licentious tongue,
My Muſe :—The KING *can do no wrong,*
We muſt not thence too much infer.
Alack! We know, His MINISTER, ⎫
And PRIVY COUNSELLORS—*can err,* ⎬
Elſe ſhould we not, as now we do, ⎭
This hateful, hopeleſs War purſue,

But

We muſt not thence too much infer.] In Abſolute Monarchies the language of ſervile adulation ſays, ' *Indigna digna habenda ſunt, REX quæ facit.*' But our maxim, that ' THE KING *can do no wrong*'—means only, that whatever may be amiſs in the conduct of public affairs is not chargeable perſonally on the KING, but on his MINISTERS.

See BLACKSTONE'S COMMENTARIES ; the beſt-digeſted Code of the beſt Laws that ever were promulgated.

This hateful, hopeleſs War.] The War with AMERICA—(in which we were engaged when I wrote this Fable)—was certainly a *hateful* one, becauſe we were fighting againſt our Kindred. Yet mean I not to adduce it as a charge of criminality againſt our then MINISTER ; certainly not. It was a War of neceſſity,—not of
choice .

But 'tis digreffing from the point :
Talking of Minifters and Kings,
And politics, and fuch like things ;
My Fable's fadly out of joint.

Yet, fhall the Gauls exemplify
How the poor RATS were doom'd to die.
E'en as when Gallic Cooks prepare,
On great occafions extra fare
For LOUIS' Court : to marfhy ground,
And ftagnant waters Paris round,
The Royal Frog-catchers refort,
On murder bent,—which they call fport.

Ev'n

choice. The outrage committed by the Boftonians, was an act of
determined Rebellion, and Defiance : it was the Guantlet AMERICA
threw down ; and we fhould have been Daftards not to have taken it
up. But,—as I approve his courage who accepts a challenge, I blame
his foolhardinefs who continues the fight when his ftrength is exhaufted,
and he has no chance of victory : or, if by miracle he fhould prove
victorious, his triumph would be but momentary ; and the conteft
muft neceffarily be renewed, and he at laft defeated. Such was our
fituation : and therefore *hopelefs* was the War.

The COLONIES were Limbs, or rather Excrefcences of the BRI-
TISH EMPIRE, out of all proportion with the Body. Sooner or later
they muft have fallen from us. What we have now to lament, is, the
manner in which they were fevered ; by dilatory operations, which
have drained us of more blood than we fhall recruit in ages.—This
mifchief—(to drop the metaphor—) feems imputable to LORD NORTH,
who neither had the fpirit requifite for carrying on a War, nor mag-
nanimity enough to make Peace.

Frog-catching fport.] It was my misfortune once to pafs a day in
a miferable Village in FRANCE, where the only Book I could meet
with

Ev'n fo the RATS GRIMALKIN chafes:
Finds out their haunts, and hiding-places:
And if upon them unawares
He pops, moft royally he fares.

So oft, indeed, by ftratagem
Feline he circumvented them;
Had it not been that fornication
Was, as at prefent 'tis, in fafhion;—
That nature and night work fupplied
Young ones, as faft as old ones died;
None had been living now to tell
How many of their brethren fell.

They fell; but not without fome vain
Attempts GRIMALKIN to reftrain.
Many a goodly projeƈt they
Effay'd; and threw much time away.

with was titled " DIVERTISSEMENTS CAMPAGNARDS." A-
mongft other goodly Diverfions, ' Frog-catching' being fet forth, I
had the curiofity to dip into it. " The Chaffeur (fays the Author)
" fhould be provided with water-proof Boots; and a Trident, or
" three-barbed Spear: for with fuch a weapon NEPTUNE ftrikes
" the Leviathan, quand il va a la Chaffe."——What a glorious
thought!—A SEA-GOD hunting Leviathans—in apt comparifon to
a BARON catching Frogs in his own Marfh!

In any other than a French Writer, I fhould have taken it for burlefque. But he feemed to be in ferious earneft. And never, I dare
fay, had he read a page of the Batrachomyomachia, though fome of
its lines correfpond in part with his defcription.

Κνημιδας μεν πρωλα περι κνημησιν εθηκαν.
Σειπλες λογχας, &c.

                                                    At

At length a City Genius hit
Upon the mode of doing it :—
Or, thinking fo ;—refolved to call
His fellow Cits to Common-Hall :—
Wafh-houfe yclept, in vulgar phrafe.
And wafh-houfe it might be o-days ;
But when the tubs were put to rights,
Served for their Common-Hall o-nights.

   Precepts were fent about the Town ;
" That every RAT in his fur gown
" Should meet one certain day—I mean
" One night."—For fear of being feen.
For though by BILL OF RIGHTS they cou'd
Meet, and talk nonfenfe when they wou'd;
GRIMALKIN watched with jealous eye
Encroachments on his Royalty.
He held that Subjects fhould incline 'em
To Kingfhip, as a *jus divinum.*
But left poor patriots fhould prate
Againft his Dignity, and State ;
Call him unthrifty, or unwife ;
And wifh to cut off his fupplies ;
He thought it well to let them know
Th' extent of duty which they owe ;—
Ev'n to their fortunes, and their blood.
If any one difpute it wou'd
He fhould find which of them the longer
Talons, or teeth had, fharper, ftronger.

                                        This

This argument the beſt that he
Could uſe to favour Tyranny,
Kept them,—(as Standing Armies do
Men-Mice,—) in awe: except a few,
Who now and then dared machinate,
And meddle with affairs of ſtate.

The Summons iſſued for a Guild
With terrour half the City fill'd.
The phraſe " On Special Bufineſs " they
Miſconſtrue one or other way.
By it the Gluttons underſtand,
Or fear a Famine in the Land:
Puzzled, what meaſures ſhould be ta'en
To regulate the price of grain.

The diſmal Politician ſtrokes
His whiſkers, ſhakes his head, and croaks.
" Flat-bottom'd Boats are coming over:—
" Hey, Brother! What's the news from DOVER ?"

The Merchant deep in others Books,
To ſome relief of *Intereſt* looks.
" Government would do well to low'r
" The uſe of caſh from five to four."
The rich one thinks ' the State ſhould fix
' The rate of intereſt at ſix.
' If 'tis a queſtion of finance,
' I *could* a plumb or two advance:—

' But

‘ *SUBSCRIPTION* bufinefs fhould it be, ⎫
‘ No doubt, they will remember me, ⎬
‘ Who have fubfcribed fo conftantly. ⎭
‘ Elfe will I openly declare
‘ How much I hate this wafteful war.
  ‘ I hate the *War.*—Yet muft I own,
‘ I love, moft dearly love a *LOAN.*
‘ *Ten per Cent* clear of brokerage paid!—
‘ But, then,—New *Taxes* muft be laid :
‘ Heavy ones, too.—But, *Ten per Cent*
‘ On Money *nominally lent*
‘ Confoles *Subfcribers.*—To be fure,—
‘ *Taxes* hurt others, Rich, and Poor.
‘ The Nation has a right to curfe
‘ The Man who holds the Public Purfe;
‘ But whilft we *favour'd Cits,* and *Men*
‘ *In Parliament* fuch profits gain,
‘ To us, at leaft, the matter 's clear,—
‘ *We* have an able Financier.’

The Man who holds the Public Purfe.] THE COMMONS are
conftitutionally the Public's Stewards; but as long as the MINISTER
can *fecure* a Majority, He is *virtually* the fole Manager.
  Amongft the many *Abufes* which MR. BURKE's admirable, and
ever-memorable BILL went to *reform,* I wonder he did not touch
upon the moft profufe expenditure of the Public's Money, and at the
fame time the moft fatal mode of Bribery that could be devifed :—
I mean—the MINISTER's difpofal of the LOANS. That he fhould
negotiate the Bufinefs is fo far fitting; but he ought to be *impeach-
able for giving it to,* and every Member fhould *forfeit his feat for
receiving*—any part of the LOAN. No MINISTER will ever want
Supporters for carrying on a War, whilft War enables him to raife
the *Wages of Corruption.*

G   The

The City RATS refolve, whate'er
The Bufinefs, to attend the May'r.

The time appointed come, they meet—
O, wonderful!—to talk ;—not eat.
The Conftables are placed about
The doors, to keep the rabble out.

Silence proclaim'd, SOREX, the May'r,
Than whom none *fill'd* fo well the Chair.
Wags his fore paws, like turtle fins ;
Hems twice,—fpits thrice,—and then begins :
  " Gemmen :—I fay :—I underftand—
  " Some weighty bufinefs—is in hand :—
  " If he be here who made requeft
  " For meeting—let him fpeak his beft."

Now rofe a pert young Alderman-
-ic RAT ; and thus his Speech began.
  ' Since by your fuffrage, Fellow Cits,—
  ' (But,—lackaday !—the May'r 's in fits.
  ' Too great exertion, as I fear,
  ' In waddling from his Manfion here
  ' Has quite exhaufted him. No wonder :
  ' With fo much flefh, fuch thick Robes under :
  ' This turtle feeding fhortens lives.
  ' Poor SOREX !—O, but—he revives.
  ' I hope, my Lord, you 're not the worfe.—
  ' Pray lend an ear to my difcourfe.)

                                    Since,

' Since, Fellow Cits, by your accord
' I was brought in for Patriot Ward,
' Whole days and nights, weeks, months and years
' I 've pafs'd opprefs'd with Public Cares.
' Awake,—afleep, —in,—out of bed,—
' The City's welfare in my head.
  ' Againft how many Scutages,
' Aids, Talliages, Carrucages,
' Have I not clamour'd loud, and long?
' 'Tis very well my lungs are ftrong.
  ' I have,—which fome will folly call,—
' Ruin'd myfelf, to ferve you all.
' So much on public bufinefs bent,
' I cared not how my fortune went.
  ' But, fince your favour ftill I boaft,
' I think my fortune lent, not loft.
' You are too generous, I 'm fure,
' To let a Patriot long be poor.
' Earneft, indeed, already you
' Have given of what you mean to do.
' And I 'm as proud to wear, as own
' The honour of this Scarlet Gown :
' Which flowing graceful from my fhoulders,
' Envy excites in all beholders.

Scutages, Talliages, &c.] Names under which the Kings of the
Norman and Saxon Lines extorted money from their Subjects.,

                         ' This

' This my firſt wiſh ambitious gain'd ;
' This ladder's lower round attain'd ;
' I flatter me ere long to mount
' Aloft, and ſet aſtride upon 't :—
' Without offence His Lordſhip to.
' The May'ralty is not my view.
' I rather would be Chamberlain ;
' And keep the City's Purſe. And then,
' If there 's no indecorum in 't,—
' I would at one more honour hint ;
' The higheſt honour you can give ;—
·' The welcomeſt I can receive ;—
' To be—your REPRESENTATIVE.
' Which once attain'd, I vow and ſwear
' To make my Country all my care :
' My zeal and lungs at conſtant work ;
' I 'll out-face Fox, and out-talk BURKE.'

Tired of his prate, a LIVERY-RAT
Kimbo'd his arms, and cock'd his hat :
" If this be all, Friend Prate-a-pace,
" *I 'm off*.—Who will may have my place."

To out-face FOX.] It is not meant to characterize MR. Fox as
an impudent, but as a bold Man :—one who dares confront any Miniſter :—one fit to be the Leader of a great Party, keeping in awe the
Servants of the Crown.

And out-talk BURKE.] Nor would I inſinuate that MR. BURKE
is ever tedious. At leaſt he was not ſo ſome years ſince, when I frequented the Houſe; (as a Gallery Man ;—*Auditor tantum.*) I have
heard him ſpeak for three hours together ; but, ſo far from thinking
he ſpoke too long, I never thought he ſpoke long enough.

' Your

‘ Your patience, worthy Sir, I pray ;—
‘ Something,——what was 't ?——I had to fay.
‘ In footh, I 'm forry to appear
‘ Tedious to any Perfon here.
‘ But this fame *Oratory* hath
‘ So many a tempting, devious path,
‘ Where Rats of Genius may for hours
‘ Amufe themfelves with culling flow'rs.——’

“ Say, rather *Talking* is a Maze,
“ Where the illogic Blockhead ftrays,
“ Without or Senfe, or Reafon's clew,
“ Or Method to direct him through.”

‘ I 'll try my beft to be concife ;
‘ And tell you, Fellows, in a trice
‘ Why I thought proper now to call
‘ You Livery here to Common Hall.
‘ The fubject is what all fhould feel ;
‘ For it imports the Common-weal :
‘ Yet, to the City's dire difgrace,
‘ We have among us fome fo bafe—
‘ They for the Public little care,
‘ Unlefs themfelves in danger are :
‘ Safe, they no meafures take to free
‘ From perils the Community.
‘ Nay more ; of their indiff'rence vain,
‘ They borrow fallacy from Men :—

“ *That*

" *That Every-body bufinefs is*
" *Nobody's :"*—vile, falfe reaf'ning this !
' A generous Rat would rather learn—
' *That every one's is his concern :*
' And would his treafures wafte and blood,
' So he could do the Public good.
' But, ah ! It would be hard to find
' Cits now of patriotic mind.
' Extinct the courage which was wont
' To animate us.—Fie upon 't !
' Luxury, and Lafcivioufnefs
' Pervade all ranks.   Ye 're fond of Drefs,
' And Revelry :—of Balls, and Feafts :
' And get as drunk as human Beafts.
    ' Unthinking wretches !—But I 'll try
' To roufe you from your lethargy.
' I 'll have a Parrot taught * to fcream—
"' *GRIMALKIN*; *Rats :—take heed of him.*
"' *GRIMALKIN!"'*—Ay ; the very fame.
' What ftart ye even at his name?
' Ye tremble, too :—I thought ye wou'd;
' For never Cat fhed fo much blood.
    ' Which of you all affembled here
' Mourns not the lofs of fome one dear ?
' But no one fo great caufe as I
' To mourn his mangled family.

* *I 'll have a Starling taught to fpeak*
  Nothing but—" MORTIMER."   SHAKSP.
                                    ' Not

‘ Not more of PRIAM's kindred died
‘ By that far-famed Trojanicide,
‘ ACHILLES, than of mine are flain
‘ Since our fell King began his reign.
‘ Such war unfeemly, too, he wages;
‘ Againft both fexes, and all ages.
‘ My Grandam, and my Grandfire eke,'
‘ The Tyrant took away laft week.
‘ Uncles, and Aunts I 've loft, and Coufins
‘ -Germain, and Irifh ones, by dozens.
‘ Saturday night, or Sunday morn
‘ My eldeft Son was from me torn :—
‘ Next day at noon his fecond Brother :—
‘ At twelve o'clock at night another.
‘ This very eve I had a Sifter;
‘ Juft as the moon uprofe I mift her.
‘ And much I fear that fell GRIMALKIN
‘ Is feafting on her whilft I 'm talking.
‘ My Wife is every day in danger:
‘ But that 's no matter,—fhe 's a Ranger;
‘ Eternal Goffiper, and Gadder :—
‘ I almoft wifh GRIMALKIN had her.
‘ His lips, I 'm told, lafcivious water
‘ No lefs to be about my Daughter.
‘ The lofs of her, too, I could bear;
‘ My Wife and Daughter I could fpare;
‘ If the fell monfter would not touch
‘ A Miftrefs whom I doat on much.

‘ Rather

‘ Rather than in his pow'r behold her,

‘ I 'll *hang his Cat-ſkin o'er my ſhoulder.* *

‘ What ſupercilious looks ye caſt !—

‘ As if my words were mere bombaſt.

‘ No; my heart 's big,—though I am little :

‘ Oh ! that I had a Spaniſh Whittle !

‘ And you ſhould ſee how I wou'd ſpoil

‘ This Cat, as MANLIUS did the Gaul.

‘ Though for my Miſtreſs' ſake, I ſaid,

‘ I wiſh'd I had a Spaniſh Blade ;

‘ Think not, my Fellow Cits, for her

‘ Alone I make this mighty ſtir.

‘ No: though my love for her is great ;—

‘ Yet, how much more I love the ſtate.

‘ I for her ſake would live ; but I

‘ Would, if the State required it, die.

‘ Though,—to be plain,—to die I 'm loath,

‘ For either ; but would live for both.

‘ And ſo I will. And ſo ſhall you

‘ All live : and unmoleſted too.

---

* *And hang a calf's-ſkin o'er thoſe recreant limbs.*　SHAKSP.

As MANLIUS *did the Gaul.*] Malice or Rivalry may call this a *mere ſhow of Learning* :—but, take my word for it, *honeſt* IAGO, our Rat is tolerably read. You will find, if you ſift him well, he is acquainted with the minuteſt circumſtances of Hiſtory. In that memorable Duel, (which cannot but remind one of the Fight betwixt DAVID and GOLIAH,) the Combatants' Weapons are particularly deſcribed. The gigantic Gaul had two Swords—" *duos Enſes;*" (probably a Sword, and Dagger:) the noble Roman had but one ; which, however, was a *Spaniſh* one :—" *Gladio Hiſpanico cinɛtus contra Gallum conſtitit.*"

‘ For

‘ For though I cannot cope with GRIM
‘ Overtly, I’ve a ſtratagem
‘ To rid us of all fears of him.
‘ For which I truſt “‘ moſt potent, grave
And reverend RATS,’” your thanks to have.

“ *Sir, you will merit more than thanks*
“ *If you can ſtop* GRIMALKIN’S *pranks.*
“ *The City’s Love—Wealth—Honours too—*”

‘ Enough, enough:—too much, Meſſieurs,’

“ *You may command. All we can do,—*”

‘ Ye are too good. That which aſſures—

“ *We ſtill ſhall be in debt to you.*”

‘ Your Love, confirms me ever yours.’

“ *Tell us the way on which you’ve hit:*
“ *Let us admire your wondrous wit..—*”

‘ Little of that. The way ’s ſo plain,
‘ I wonder I could rack my brain
‘ So many ſleepleſs nights in vain.
‘ Not that I grudge my labour paſt;
‘ Since I have compaſs’d it at laſt.
‘ I’ll tell you how it may be done,
‘ And frame a motion thereupon.

H   ‘ Liſt,

' Lift, then, all parties, all connexions,
' RATS of all ages and complexions:
' Whisker'd, or not: black, white, and grey,
' Liften to what I have to fay.

A murmur ran through all the croud.
Some noify Coxcombs who ftood near him
Impertinently bawl'd aloud—
    " *The Motion, Motion : hear him, hear him.*"

' GRIMALKIN'S great advantage lies
' In fpringing on us by furprize:
' When we are thoughtlefs, carelefs, fporting;
' Or wrangling, jangling; fighting; courting.
' Whether a-bed, or up we are;
' Feafting, or fafting; or at pray'r:
' He comes upon us unaware.
' So that, my Fellows,—to prevent
' Henceforward fuch like accident,
' All that is wanting is *to hear*
' GRIMALKIN ere he gets too near.
' Now, as no time is to be loft,
' I move—THAT AT THE CITY'S COST
' BE MADE A SILVER BELL; AND PUT
' FORTHWITH GRIMALKIN'S NECK ABOUT.
' By this mean he can ne'er ftir out
' But we muft hear him: and 'twill be
' Signal for us away to flee.'

                                    Thus,

Thus, zealous in the common caufe,
The *City Politician* fpake :
And the RATS thunder'd fuch applaufe
As made the very wafh-tubs fhake.

Soon as the Chairman could compofe
Their joy tumultuous, up rofe
A RAT whofe venerable front,
Had but few ftraggling hairs upon 't ;
And white ones : for, like NESTOR, he
Had lived through generations three :
But—without his loquacity.
Our RAT was wifer ; for he knew
Long fpeeches are ill liften'd to. .
Therefore in giving his advice
He always ftrove to be concife.
Whene'er he rofe, great Rats, and fmall
Sat down, and were attentive all.

" This goodly projeft of a BELL
" Is plaufible : it likes you well.
 " But—I am loath your joy to check ;—
" When the BELL 's made, where will be found
" The Hero that dares tie it round
 " The terrible GRIMALKIN's neck ?"

Would

Would not this Fable, think you, suit
A certain modern Machiavel,
  Who waking dreams—
  And sleeping schemes
Things that it is impossible
For such a Mouse to execute?

F A B L E   XVI.

H E R M E S, *and the* S H A D E S.

AS HERMES from this World's abode
    Drove on a flock of SHADES to Hell,*
A party of them on the road
    Thus into converſation fell.

' Poor ALTAMONT !—(A FEMALE ſpeaks.)—
  ' A truer Lover none e'er had.
' Methinks, I hear ev'n yet his ſkrieks.
  ' My loſs, alaſs! will drive him mad.'

" Much worſe *my* loſs is felt:—(replies
  A MASTER OF A FAMILY.)—
" My Widow 's weeping out her eyes:
  " My Children fain would follow me."

''' Some individuals o'er your ſod
  ''' May drop a tear:—(A GENERAL ſaid:)—
''' But o'er the Public's Demi-God
  ''' The Nation tears profuſe will ſhed.'''

---

* The HELL, HADES, or LOWER WORLD of the Ancients
compriſed the whole of the Regions which were the receptacle of de-
parted Perſons; of the good as well as of the bad. And it was
the province of HERMES to conduct them there.

                                                      '''' Your

"" Your Nation fingly—(fays a BARD)—
"" Might grieve for you; but when *I* died,
"" Then univerfal groans were heard:
"" The World with grief grew ftupified.""

HERMES no longer could forbear
  From laughing. ' By my wand, fays he,
' The moft conceited Souls ye are
  ' That ever left mortality.

' To hear you talk, one would fuppofe
  ' You were of fo much confequence,
' That with the World above it goes
  ' Strangely, fince you were driven thence.

' Know;—Firft, fair DAME,—the Lover whom
  ' You creduloufly thought fo true,
' Has got a Miftrefs in your room:
  ' And doats on her, as erft on you.

' You,—who a HUSBAND, and a FATHER
  ' Of fuch fond Children boaft yourfelf,
' Know, they are by the ears together:
  ' And fond of nothing but your pelf.

' Your Widow would, perhaps, lament
  ' Your lofs; be inconfolable;—
' But that her Milliner has fent
  ' Home Mourning fhe becomes fo well.

                              ' As

' As for your character,—your worth,
  ' GENERAL DEMI-GOD ;—they fay,
' There 's not your fellow upon earth
  ' For prudence ; —for you ran away.

' Though fpoken of invidioufly
  ' By fome ; as if you mifbehaved :
' No *captured* General can deny—
  ' Your army and yourfelf you faved.

' You, the great GENIUS of your age,—
  ' The MÆVIUS, BAVIUS,—or who not?
' The Public's thoughts you fo engage,—
  ' Your Works already are forgot.

' Had you all been of merit tried ;
  ' And every praife entitled to ;—
' The World is too much occupied,
  ' To throw away a thought on you.'

        In footh, it matters not a whit,
          When a few Men or Pifmires die ;
        Jove has fo wifely order'd it,
          Nature fills up the vacancy.

                                    F A B L E

F A B L E . XVII.

The CIRCUMSPECT TRAVELLER.

A Man who had a River ſtrange to paſs,
Fathom'd, to find where fordable it was;
And, conſtantly, in doing ſo, he found
Where it ran noiſeleſs it was moſt profound.

'Tis ſo in life: We ſafely may infer
That he is ſhalloweſt who makes moſt ſtir.
Brave Men are cool: Wiſe Men avoid debate.—
But Cowards bluſter ; and Half-Idiots prate.

FABLE

F A B L E XVIII.

The SENTIMENTAL DOVE and the SPARROW.

A Brisk, young SPARROW fell in love
With an affected TURTLE-DOVE:
And meeting with her one May-day,
Alone, upon a myrtle spray,
The wanton rogue began to bill,
And force her to his wicked will.
    But, she, reserved as e'er was prude,
Chid him for offering to be rude.
' Such forward doings ne'er will move her:
' She 's for a *sentimental* Lover.
' None other shall her heart enthrall:
' 'Tis *Sentiment* is All in All.'

    SPARROW replies,—" I've often heard
" Of this same fine, high-sounding word ;
" But never yet knew what it meant:
" Explain;—what is this *Sentiment ?*"

    ' It is,—it is,—nor more nor less—;
' What I want language to exprefs:
' But, happy, happy he possessing
' So great, so rich, so sweet a blessing!
                    I   " And

" And, pray, who knows but I poſſeſs
" This well-defined—*nor more nor leſs* ;—
" This ſweet, rich, luſcious quality?
" It may be worth your while to try."

' *You* bleſs'd with it !'

       " Nay; never flout,
" Untill you find I am without.
" If not with *Sentiment* endued,
" I've qualities, perhaps, as good.
 " Imprimis, Dear; were you my wife,
" I would be conſtant all my life.
" You, and you only would careſs
" From night till morning ;—more or leſs ;—
" As you might be in humour for 't :
" For SPARROW though, and fond of ſport,
" I am withal a Bird diſcreet ;
" And can forbear till you think meet.
" Happy if with officious beak
" I may your ruffled feathers ſleek ;
" Or other office what you pleaſe,—
" Ev'n to the catching of your fleas.
" For, greater pleaſure can we prove
" Than tending upon thoſe we love?
" And you and I, ſweet Bird, will be
" Proverbial for felicity.
 " What ſays my Fair ?—Are you content?
" Is this what you call *Sentiment ?*"

            The

The Dove affectedly replies,
(With drawn-in bill, and half-fhut eyes;)
‘ This looks, indeed, like *Sentiment*;
‘ But not fo to its full extent.
‘ No; that is ftill a fomething more:—
‘ Platonic Love.—Which I adore.
‘ ’Tis Love—from fenfual joys refined:
‘ A Love—peculiar to the mind.’

“ ’Tis very well; (the SPARROW cries;)
“ Half words are whole ones to the wife.
“ Your illuftration ’s clear and ftriking:—
“ *Cock Sparrows are not to your liking.*
“ So, fare you well: I’ll try to find
“ Elfewhere fome feather’d one more kind.”

With this; a carelefs bow he made;
And lightly flapp’d his wings, and fled.

Ere out of hearing he had foar’d,
She call’d him back—

     ‘ One little word, ’
‘ Sweet Sir.—What was ’t, I would have faid?
‘ Plague o’ this fwimming in my head!
‘ So dim my eyes, I fcarce can fee:—
‘ Dear SPARROW, do take hold of me.
 ‘ Whilft I’ve yet ftrength I’ll try to clamber,
‘ With your affiftance, to my chamber.

       ‘ And

‘ And when I'm fafe in bed you may,—
‘ If you think proper,—go away.’

Some Dames there are fo very whimfical,
  With fupercilioufnefs they treat *.
Impaffion'd Lovers, proftrate when they fall,
  And fue for favours at their feet.

With fuch—affect indifference.   Pretend
  A willingnefs to go; and they
Become fo facile, they will condefcend
  Ev'n to follicit you to ftay.

* Ardeat ipfa licet, tormentis gaudet Amantis.
                                    JUVENAL.

FABLE

F A B L E   XIX.

The HOUSE-DOG, and the WOLF.

WHO that the fweets of *LIBERTY* does know,
On any terms that bleſſing would forego?

A lean, half-famiſh'd WOLF, that chanc'd to ſtray
Near a Court-yard towards the break of day,
Saw through the grate a MASTIFF ſleek and fat.
They wagg'd their tails, and enter'd into chat.
" Whofe Houſe is this?"
         ' SQUIRE RUSTIC's, Sir. You feem
' A ſtranger here;—not to have heard of him!'

" I never heard him mention'd in my life."

' Nor MADAM RUSTIC:—his fine-lady Wife?
' Have you ne'er heard it faid, ſhe has undone
' The SQUIRE by play:—and quarrell'd with his Son?
' 'Tis wonderful Men will difturb their lives,
' When happy Widowers, with Second Wives!'

" Thefe things are fecrets which ne'er reach'd my ears:
" Nor care I about other folks affairs."

' What!—Not for other peoples' fecrets care!
' In footh, Sir, you are very fingular.
                      ' Do

' Do you not go to any Skittle-ground,
' Gambling, or Public-houfe ? We've many round
' The country ; whereto idle Dogs refort
' And kill their time with various kinds of fport,
' And mifchief ; till at laft they're tuck'd up for't.'

    " Not fuch my life : inhabiting a wood,
" I feldom quit it, but in fearch of food."

    ' What ! can you pafs your evenings away
' Without or tippling, goffiping, or play ?
' I know no Dogs that can :—and in my eyes,
' A Dog you feem, though of a larger fize,
' And fiercer look. Unkempt, indeed, as yet
' Your hair ; and rough your coat : but when you get
' Into good keeping, you will look as well,
' As fat, as fleek as I.'

                 " Ay ?—Prithee, tell
" How I can grow as portly as you are :
" You look as if you fed on dainty fare."

    ' Excellent truly. And fo, Friend, may you,
' Feed on like fare,—if you'll like fervice do.'

    " What kind of fervice, pray, Sir, may it be ?
" I'm ftrong enough ; no work will frighten me."

    ' What you've to do is trifling, next to play ;—
' 'Tis only to fright houfe-breakers away
' By night, and let in vifitors by day.'

                                 " If

" If that be all the bufinefs, I embrace
" It gladly. Can you help me to a place?"

' Perchance. Our Neighbour's Porter, as they fay,
' Died of an apoplexy t'other day.
' If no one yet is to his place preferr'd,
' I'll afk our Butler to put in a word.'

" O! what a life luxurious fhall I lead!
" And not, as heretofore, in daily need:
" Summer 'and winter forced abroad to roam
" For food, full many a weary mile from home:
" Precarious fare. But now, O, grateful change!
" For pleafure only I abroad fhall range:
" And when at home, be regularly fed:
" Lay foft: and have a covering o'er my head.
" Some care I'll take of this fweet perfon, too:
" And wear a gloffy coat, as well as you."

Thus joy'd in thought, he chanced to caft his eye
On the Dog's neck; and afks impatiently,—
" But hey-day!—What has made this *circle*, pray,
" About your neck?—The hair is worn away.
" Have you with other Maftiff lately fought?
" Or have you in a gin or fnare been caught?—
" For 'tis too regularly mark'd, to be
" A fighting fcar.—Explain it, pray, to me."

' Pooh!—'Tis a trifling circumftance; a thing
' Of no import: 'tis not worth mentioning.'

                                        " I crave

" I crave your pardon ; but, your being fhy
" Of telling, ftirs my curiofity."

' Why, then, I'll tell you, Friend, (fince I muft fpeak)
' I fometimes wear a Collar round my neck.'

" A *Collar !* What is that ?—And what to do ?"

' A leather thong, annex'd a chain unto ;
' Which, with a ftaple driven in the wall,
' Confines me, that' ——— ,

         " You fcarce can wag at all :
" I underftand you ; I have feen a chain ;
" And Dogs, too, tugging to get loofe, in vain.
" So, Sir, your Servant : I'll trot home again."

' Why in fuch hafte ?'

         " The place will not agree
" With my proud fpirit. No : I muft be free.
" Though almoft ftarved, myfelf I ne'er could bring
" To wear a Collar : 'tis a fervile thing :
" The chain yet worfe : and then, to be confined !—
" The very thought of it appals the mind."

' Imagined ills ! The Collar 's no difgrace.
' And, though confin'd,—'tis in a cleanly place.
' Nor am I chain'd but with my own good will.'

" Oh ! worfe, and worfe :—what let 'em ufe you ill !
" Would not a Beaft of fpirit fooner die ?
" But you, tame wretch, feem pleafed with flavery.

            " You.

" You own a Mafter : crouch at his command :
" And fawn, I dare to fay, and lick his hand
" Ev'n whilft he 's chaining you."

                                        ' And what of that ?
' See you how well I'm recompenfed ? How fat
' I am ? I thrive at leaft beneath his care.
' I'm daily fed with fuch delicious fare
' As, Mr. Barebones, faucy as you be,
' You would be very glad to fhare with me.
' Stay, but, and fee the breakfaft they will bring.
' A *Slave*, indeed !—I feaft me like a *King*.'

  " My fervice to your King-fhip.   May you be
" Feafted alone : the place will not fuit me.
" No :—I'm a WOLF. I'd rather *lean* remain,
" And *free* ;—than a *fat* DOG, and wear a *Chain*."

K

FABLE

F A B L E XX.

The ZEBRA *and the* HORSE.

A ZEBRA infolent, and proud,
   Kept in the King's Menagery,
Vaunting, as oft he did, aloud,—
   ' None had fo fine a coat as he.'

" True!—(Says the HACKNEY of a Squire,
   Who chanced along that road to pafs :)
" Your gaudery we muft admire :—
   " But, ftill, we know you for an *ASS.*"

FABLE XXI.

The TWO PEARS.

TWO PEARS, upon adjacent trees, (who talk'd
Much as School-Miffes did who near them walk'd,)
Difcourfing earneftly, ONE faid—' That fhe,
' Though younger, was the riper ; and would be
' Gather'd the firft.'

     " I'll not for forwardnefs
" Difpute ; (the OTHER faid :) I am the lefs :
" But mark me well, my Friend :—if you're not gotten
" Off in good time, you'll *fpoil.—Soon ripe, foon rotten.*"

F A B L E

FABLE XXII.

The DRONES, and the BEE,

A Set of silly, City DRONES,
    Indolent, good-for-nothing ones,
Idly refolved on an excurfion
To WINDSOR; for a week's diverfion.
And, that they might be fure to pafs
Their time well, each would take a Lafs,
If fine the weather, they would ramble
About the Parks: elfe, drink, and gamble,
  But, not content with being bad
Themfelves, they 'd fain draw in a Lad—
(Oaf that I am!)—I mean a BEE,
To make one of the company.
  Th' induftrious BEE excufes made:
" His time was taken up in Trade.
" Nor had he relifh, more than leifure,
" For parties of *fuch* fort of pleafure.
" *Gambling* he did not underftand:
" He ne'er took dice, nor cards in hand.
" No joy to him the being *drunk.*
" Nor had he any favourite *Punk.*

" To

" To say the truth,—not yet was he
" Initiated in venery.
" His strength he would not idly waste:
" But would, whilst Bachelor, be chaste;
" That, if he e'er should married be,
" He might have healthful progeny."

The DRONES were thunderstruck to hear
So young a Cato—so severe.
For every syllable he spoke
Seem'd against them a levell'd stroke
Of Satire. Doubtless, for their sakes,
He cried down Gamesters—Drunkards—Rakes.
Which so exasperated them,
That with revenge they threaten'd him.
Boldly avow'd—' they would devise
' Mischief: and not ev'n stick at lies.
' For if to punishment they cou'd
' Bring him by any means, they wou'd.
' They'd swear he had done this,—done that;—
' Honey purloin'd;—and—Jove knows what.—
' Which when his Mistress heard of, he
' Excluded from the Hive would be.'

To which the BEE made this reply:
" Your utmost malice I defy.
" My gracious Mistress is not one
" Easy to be imposed upon.

" She

" She will fift well the truth, and weigh
" My merits againft all you fay.
" And, I've no doubt, my character
" Will countervail what you aver.
" But,—ev'n if falfhood fhould prevail
" For once :—Should fhe believe the tale;—
" Should fhe difgrace me :—ay ;—or drive
" With ignominy from the Hive ;—
" That, though a punifhment fevere,—
" Or death itfelf undaunted I could bear,
" My *confcience* being from offences *clear*."

F A B L E XXIII.

The W O L F and the L A M B.

A WOLF, and LAMB at the fame inftant came
To flake their thirft at a pellucid ftream.
Although the WOLF ftood higher, tow'rds the fource,
The water flowing undifturb'd, of courfe,
To him,—refolved to quarrel,—he began
To tax the LAMB: complain'd the water ran
Muddy from him: and wonder'd—' He fhould dare
' Difturb it, when he faw his Wolf-fhip there.'

" With great fubmiffion, Sir,—how can it be?—
" Does not the water run from you to me?"

' Another thing; pert Sir.—I fain would know
' Why you abufed me?'

" When?"

' Six months ago.'

" Whoever told you fo, a falfehood told:
" For, Sir, I am not yet a quarter old."

' If 't was not you, it was your Father, then.'

The LAMB, with filial piety, would fain
Have clear'd his Father's character:—in vain:—

For

For at one fpring the WOLF, blood-thirfty Brute,
Seized on the LAMB; and ended the difpute.

    Thus Kings, and Nobles, in defpotic Land,
Grafp the poor Peafantry with ruthlefs hand.

    But,—happy Countrymen! How blefs'd our ftate:
Unawed, unfhackled by the Proud, or Great.
Here to the Commonalty Law affords
Protection againft too imperious Lords.
Not ev'n the King in power is fo ftrong—
To dare to do his meaneft Subject wrong.
I do not mean, our prefent Monarch *would*.—
I know he would not do fo, if he could.
Still, to be free, regard with jealous eye
The leaft encroachments of Authority.
    But, above all, a STANDING ARMY dread.
If once that Monfter rears too high its head;—
If e'er our military force fhould be
Augmented much, we rifk our Liberty.
· The danger is not now; nor is it near;
I truft: but, diftant ages, (fhould they hear
My fmall, weak voice,) the precept will revere
No lefs; nor hold their birthright—Liberty—lefs dear.

F A B L E XXIV.

Two Dogs *fighting for a Bone.*

TWO Dogs, the fierceft of their kind,
Happen'd a Bacon Bone to find :
One quickly feized upon the Bone ;
Which 't Other claim'd ;—' Leave that alone :
' 'Tis mine : I faw it before you.'

" 'T were hard to prove if that be true.
" But, whiche'er faw it firft, or laft,
" I have it : and I 'll hold it faft."

' Sirrah ! I fay, take off your paw.
' Or halve it : or I 'll go to Law.
' 'Tis written—"' *Rebus de inventis'*"——'

" Nonfenfe !—I fay,—"' *Jus poffidentis'*"——
" But 't were loft time to hold difpute
" With fuch a known-litigious Brute ;
" Therefore, to cut the matter fhort,
" Give up your claim, or fight me for 't."

' Ay ; that I will, with all my heart,
' Notorious Bruifer though thou art,
' Thou canft not frighten me. I 'll fight
' Rather than give up what 's my right.'

Or halve it :] Δεινος απαιτησαι το μερ☉,—κοινον ειναι
Φησας τον Ερμην.   Theophr.

L   Thus

Thus faid; the Champions ftraight engag'd;
And long, and furious combat waged;
So much, the ground whereon they ftood
Could not drink faft enough their blood.
And had not channels ten, or fewer,
Carried it to the common fewer,
Our Combatants had both been found
In no-*pacific* ocean drown'd.

(Should any one devoid of tafte,
Call this difcription ' mere bombaft ;'—
Abufe the pun : and wonder how
I dare fuch latitude allow
Myfelf :—CALLIOPE maintains—
((Thank you, dear Goddefs, for the pains
Of vindicating what *I* 've done—
Or rather *you* ;—but that 's all one :
((('Tis fit the world at large fhould know it,
I am her tragi-comic Poet.
WALLBECKOMASTIX if there be
Any will this difpute with me,
Let him draw forth his—*grey goofe Quill* ;
Whilft I 've a drop of—*ink*, I will
Fight with him : ay ; and make him caper,
Until he 's tired of it, on —— *paper*.
With other fighting what have *I*
To do? My field—is *Poetry* ;
My fword—my *Pen*. Not willingly
Draw it I would in enmity :

But,

But, if compell'd to draw at all,
Take heed ; for it is dipp'd in gall :
And never Indian's poifon'd dart
With deadlier virus touch'd the heart.)))
But, now ; may 't pleafe your Goddefs-fhip,
Proceed : nor let th' occafion flip
Of fetting forth the dignity
Of this our currifh Epopee.
((((Silence, ye noify Sons of Earth !
Heaven-born CALLIOPE holds forth.))))
""" *Let no one pafs harfh judgement on*
""" *This Poem worthy Helicon.*
""" *Far from burlefque, 'tis true fublime,*
""" *Purpofely broken, to give time*
""" *For two fuch valiant Curs to fight.*
""" *This 'tis to* think, *as well as write.*
""" *Some Authors would have fcribbled on*
""" *The Story ; and have got all done,*
""" *Ere my lov'd Bard had finifh'd this*
""" *Quadripartite parenthefis.'"*)

Long fought the Dogs ; and fought fo well
It was impoffible to tell
Which had the better. Void of ftrength
They fell together at full length.

Juft then, as they exhaufted lay,
Motionlefs, breathlefs,—cunning TRAY,
(Who at a diftance watch'd the fray,)
Stepp'd in,—*and took the Bone away,*

ENGLAND

ENGLAND and FRANCE for *Commerce* go to War.
Ye jealous Nations, will ye ne'er be wife?
By your Diffentions NEUTRALS vantaged are.
You wafte your ftrength, *They* carry off the Prize.

The MOTHER COUNTRY's right of controul over her own CO-
LONIES, was ENGLAND's juftification in the late War with NORTH
AMERICA. FRANCE took part with the Americans; and the rea-
fon LEWIS THE SIXTEENTH gave, to juftify his breach with Us,
was the moft *curious* and *ridiculous* one that a weak and infolent
Monarch ever gave,—namely, *his Love of Liberty.—He,* LEWIS THE
SIXTEENTH,—holding his *own* Subjects in the moft *abject Slavery*,—
pretended all of a fudden an enthufiaftic fondnefs for *general Freedom.*
I fhould be apt here to exclaim in the oft-cited words of HORACE,—
" *Rifum teneatis, Amici ?*"—but that I am fure no honeft Englifh-
man's indigation has yet fubfided. If, centuries hence, our pofterity,
reading the *Manifefto* of LEWIS THE SIXTEENTH, fhould be be-
trayed into a fmile, it will be—the fmile of *ineffable contempt.*

But whatever the Manifeftos of either Court might fet forth,—
whatever might be the *alleged* reafons for the War, every child in
politics knows, that the *real* motive to it was the hope of poffeffing
the *Commerce* with AMERICA folely and exclufively. That was, in
reality, the *Bone of Contention.* And whilft We, (ENGLAND and
FRANCE,) were ruining ourfelves by the conteft,—RUSSIA, DEN-
MARK, SWEDEN, and HOLLAND, (till She was herfelf engaged,) and
all the NEUTRAL POWERS of Europe were profiting by our folly.

I wrote this FABLE in the year 1782, when we were actually at
War. Since that time *Peace* has happily been re-eftablifhed: and the
Minifter is endeavouring to ftrengthen its bands by a *commercial* Intercourfe with FRANCE. I have not fo irreconcilable a hatred to the
French, as to be forry to have any communication with them;—but,—
timeo Danaos et dona ferentes.—I fufpect the French Cabinet of
entering into this Treaty with the political view—*of throwing us off
our guard.*

National Reflections caft upon fimple Individuals are often cruel,
and always illiberal; but in reference to States, they are generally
juft: for, almoft every Nation has its characteriftic qualities. Were
I to fay thofe of FRANCE are *Cunning, Duplicity,* and *Perfidiouf-
nefs*;—the Hiftory of many Ages would warrant the affertion.—
But

But to come immediately to our own days ;—Does not the *reigning Monarch*, and the *reigning Minifter* of FRANCE poſſeſs thoſe very qualities in an eminent degree ? I appeal to the memory of every Man living in Europe, and to the faƈt, of FRANCE's interference in the late War. MONSIEUR DE VERGENNES, the preſent Miniſter, did, in the name of LOUIS SEIZE, the preſent French King, give us the ſtrongeſt *profeſſions* of Friendſhip, at the breaking out of,— and ſome time after the War had been carried on againſt AMERICA. Whereas all the while He was abetting the Americans ; and from the firſt was fully reſolved to break with us. He waited only till he had lulled our then Miniſter into a fooliſh, and almoſt fatal ſecurity ; and then he opened upon us ſuch a tremendous naval battery, as aſtoniſhed, and *almoſt frightened* ſome of our oldeſt Commanders. " *Cui bono*,—to what purpoſe, (ſays the Reader,) this long political Note ?"

Patience, good Sir ; You ſhould know, I am neither a Spouter in Parliament, nor a Holder-forth in Coffee-Heuſes, nor yet a Pamphleteer, nor a Paragraph Writer ; do then afford me the only opportunity I have of leƈturing the Old Miniſtry, and adviſing the New. If, like many of my Brothers of the Quill, I write, and write, and nobody reads, that is not my fault. I *would* ſave the Nation.— Not by oppoſing the Commercial Syſtem : No ; I hope, if carried into effeƈt, it will anſwer the good intentions of MR. PITT. But I hope, and truſt it will not anſwer the political purpoſe of the COURT OF VERSAILLES,—to make us relax our Vigilance. Whilſt, indeed, THE KING has the *ableſt Seaman* in the World, the *brave* and *indefatigable* LORD HOWE, to co-operate with MR. PITT, the Nation has not much to fear. His profeſſional, as well as perſonal ſpirit is our guarantee, that he will not hold the office of FIRST LORD OF THE ADMIRALTY upon any other terms, than, *keeping up a great Naval Force.*

It is a found maxim in Politics, to make Peace with the *ſword drawn*; that is, not to ſuſpend hoſtilities during the negotiation. It is no leſs politic to keep arms within one's reach, when Peace *is* made.

I would not walk in any Street in Italy with a ſworn Foe, without having my hand upon my ſword. And though he ſhould throw away his oſtenſible weapon, and profeſſing a friendſhip for me, approach to *traffic*, yet would I keep an eye upon him, and, ſuſpicious of a *lurking dagger*, be prepared for the worſt. Nations are but Individuals in aggregate. Whatever it may be wiſe in theſe to obſerve, it will be fooliſh in thoſe to negleƈt.

FABLE

F A B L E   XXV.

The T w o W a l l e t s.

JOVE, when he framed us, had in mind
    Our Blifs; and gave us Wallets two.
Our *Faults* in one we fling behind:
Our *Virtues* we keep full in view.

THE inconvenience which attends
    Our mode of wearing them is this,
We fee the failings of our friends,—
But nothing in ourfelves amifs.

F A B L E   XXVI.

The L e o p a r d, *and the* F o x.

A LEOPARD boafting of ' his beauteous Skin;'—
    A Fox replied,—" My merit lies *within*."

F A B L E   XXVII.

The T o r t o i s e, *and the* E a g l e.

A Tortoise, not content that he could fwim
    In water well; and on the land could crawl;
Seeing an Eagle *fly*, entreated him
    To take him up;—He did; and—let him fall.

WHEN Folk ambitious quit their proper fphere,
No wonder if their folly cofts them dear.

FABLE

F A B L E   XXVIII.

The DAW *in Peacocks Feathers.*

IS it not laughable to fee
Young Philpot, after fhutting fhop,
Give himfelf airs in company ;—
And ftrut about ; and play the Fop ?

Gossipina fhows off at Bath.
Is there a Duchefs in the Rooms
More coftly cloaths ;—more diamonds hath ;—
A longer train ;—or higher plumes ?

KILL'D by inclemency of weather,
A Peacock ftretch'd upon the ground,
By a Jack-Daw was found,
And ftripp'd of every feather.
Straight he bedecks him with the gaudy plumes ;
And a majeftic, lofty port affumes.

Upon Hydafpes' bank he ftood,
Admiring much his perfon in the flood,
Which ferved him for a looking-glafs.
Wide he expands his variegated tail,
And mimics, (as he thinks,) fo well
The grace of Juno's Bird, he has no doubt
But, thus deck'd out,
He for her favourite any where would pafs.

Unluckily

Unluckily for poor Jack-Daw,
  A flock of Peacocks came to drink
- At the fame River's brink,
And their ftrange counterfeited-fellow faw.

Inftead of fkulking to fome tree,
Or hole, to hide his gaudery;
Proud of what aukwardly he wore,
The graceful Birds he ftruts before:
Nay, even prefumes with them to mix.
Round him they throng; and fix
    Their eyes indignantly on him:
    And clamour loud; and fcream.

One, more farcaftic than the reft,
  Says, (meaning to be overheard,)
  ' Do any of you know this Bird?
' How vulgarly the Thing is dreft!'

Another Peacock, fond of fun,
Propofed,—" He fhould be made to run
" The gantlet." "" Ay.—Agreed upon.""

The Daw the propofition heard:
More pale.he grew at every word.
But when the preparations dire,—
    The ranks a-forming beaks a-whetting,
Stern vifages, and eyes on fire,
    He faw,—refolved upon retreating.

He ftrove to get away; in vain :
   Encumber'd with his finery,
   The haplefs caitiff could not fly :
Was taken ; and brought back again.

The difcipline fevere began :
Poor JACK the gantlet ran,
   With his beft hafte ;—
   Yet·not fo faft ;—
     But ere 't was done,
He of his borrow'd feathers, every one,
Was ftripp'd ; and no fmall portion of his own.

Abafh'd, confounded, home he goes ;
   Curfing the Peacocks : and relates
   The ufage to his old Affociates.
And to enfure compaffion, fhows
   His body bruifed, his pinions bare.
Inftead of pitying, they one and all
   Rally the Blockhead ; and declare
   ' That moft fincerely glad they are—
' *His pride, his odious pride, has had a fall.*'

F A B L E XXIX.

The LION feigning Sickness.

LEO grown lazy, old, or lame,
His Houfehold were ill off for game;
Or eatables of any fort.
Allowances ran very fhort.
Save the hind quarters of a Horfe;
An Afs's brifket, tough and coarfe;
Part of a Stag; and half a Boar;
Little contain'd the larder more.

For which, his Caterer and Cook,
JACKAL, occafion proper took,
Humbly to tell his Majefty,
He ftood in need of a fupply.
‘ Your Houfehold, Sire, and all your Train
‘ Of their lank carcafes complain.
‘ May I prefume to name the *Queen?*—
‘ I grieve to fee fhe grows fo lean.
‘ And, which of all her *Maids-of-Honour*
‘ Has half an ounce of flefh upon her?
‘ Your *Chaplains*—(if fuch idle Drones
‘ Thrive not, how fhould induftrious ones
‘ Whofe labour wears them to the bones?)—
‘ Your *Chaplains* moft devoutly pray
‘ For better viands every day.

. ‘ The

' The *Beef-eaters* beg leave to join
' In fuch a prayer; and hope to dine
' A little oftener on Sirloin. }

   ' But why enumerate every one?—
' They're famifh'd all.'

                 " What 's to be done?—
(The LION fays.)   " I cannot hunt
" So frequently as I was wont.
" And yet I fhould be forry that
" My Houfehold were not fleek and fat."

   ' May 't pleafe you, Sire; I know a trick
' Might anfwer.—*Make believe you 're fick.*
' All forts of Beafts will then refort,
' Or out of grief, or joy, to Court.
' And when we have them fafe within
' The coop, let 's kill 'em, fat and lean.'

   The King approves the fcheme: and fends
His Pages round, as well to Friends,
As to inveterate Enemies:
To fay,—"" In abject ftate he lies:
"" By Doctors given o'er. And he
"" Wifhes his Subjects all to fee:
"" To be forgiven paft injuries
"" Of every fort, before he dies.
"" For, till forgiven by all Brute-kind,
"" He cannot die in peace of mind.""

                                  Of

Of all the Beasts to whom they sent
Of none were they so diffident
As of the Fox: they knew that he,
Remarkable for subtilty,
Was not, as senseless boobies are,
Easy to draw into a snare.
 They therefore to the message add,—
“‘ The dying Monarch would be glad
“‘ Of his advice; to make his Will
“‘ Anew; or add a Codicil.
“‘ Earnestly beg him,—not to stay
“‘ To dress himself; but trot away:
“‘ For they (the APES) were in a fright,
“‘ Lest he should not live out the night.’”

 RENARD express'd ‘ his grief at hearing
‘ The King to t'other world was steering:
‘ But hoped he would not pass the Styx
‘ Before he called.   He could not fix
‘ The time: for possibly it might
‘ Be late; or not at all that night.
‘ But the next morning, certainly
‘ He 'd wait upon His Majesty.’

 The morning came; Fox never went:
Nor next, nor next: nor ever meant:
Till business calling him abroad,
He took the Palace in his road.
 Far as the vestibule he ventured;
Look'd in; but prudently not enter'd.

LEO,

LEO, who had not ftirr'd from home,
Was overjoy'd to fee him come.
He bade his Apes go forth to meet him ;
With falutations many greet him.
"" They wonder'd that they had not feen
"" Him fooner :—that the King had been
"" Enquiring after him ; and was
"" Afraid that illnefs was the caufe
"" Of his long abfence. But 't would cheer ⎫
"" The good old King at length to hear ⎬
"" The voice of one he held fo dear.— ⎭
"" For as to feeing him,—poor Soul !—
"" LEO was blinder than a Mole.'"
Artful as was the Pages' fpeech,
The Fox they could not over-reach.

With much grimace, and bows and fcrapes,—
In their own coin he pays the APES.
' He did but call as he went by,
' To know how fared his Majefty.
' Great JOVE he fervently petitions
' To fave him, fpite of his Phyficians.'

"" You muft not go. What will the King
"" Think of fo very ftrange a thing ?
"" It looks fo like difloyalty,
"" I dare not tell him.'" " No ; nor I :
" I'm very fure, fhould he furvive,
" Such treatment he will not forgive."

The

The Fox continues obſtinate,
Not to ſet foot within the gate.

LEO, who liſtening overheard
The altercation, every word,
Exclaims—" What ! RENARD ?—Pray draw near.
" I 've ſomething for your private ear :
" Matter moſt intricate, and nice.
" I ſtand in need of your advice
" Touching my will.   The whelp, my Heir,
" Is thoughtleſs,—young :—you underſtand.
" Your parchment ;—come,—take quill in hand."

' Sire, I have brought nor ſtamps, nor quill
' Along with me.   Defer your Will,
' So pleaſe you, to another day.'

" Well, be it ſo.   But, ſtep this way.
" There 's ſomething elſe on which I 'd ſpeak
" To you.——Ay, me !—I grow ſo weak,
" That every time I fetch my breath
" I feel I'm drawing nearer death."

' Sire, you had better talk no longer :
' Wait till you get a little ſtronger.'

" Well ; we'll not talk : but do walk in.
" It is an age ſince I have ſeen
" Any one of your family.

                                    " I'd

" I 'd fain confer, before I die,
" Some favour on you.   Wealth,—or Land,—
" Or what?"

        ' None ; fave to kifs your hand.
. ' For which I would approach your bed,
' Might I be fo far honoured.————
    ' Foh !—what does this rank odour mean ?
' Your Nurfes do not keep you clean ;
' I fear.   Or do your Butchers treat
' Your Majefty with ftinking meat?
    ' I muft retire.   I cannot bear
' Longer to breathe fuch noxious air.'

    " If that 's the cafe.—(the King replies,)
" I 'll try if I have ftrength to rife :—
" For fpeak with you, I muft, fweet Sir."

    ' Not for the world.   You fhall not ftir.
' 'T would be a fhame, fhould it be faid,
' For *me* you ventured out of bed.
' No ; no :—lay ftill, and keep you warm :
' The chilly air will do you harm.
    ' For fear of mifchief, which would grieve
' Me very much,—I take my leave.'

    " Stop ; fays the Lion.   Ere you go,
" Refolve one thing.   I fain would know,
" Why you fo long have kept away ?—
" And now feem fearful of foul-play?

                  " Has

" Has any one my fcheme betray'd ?
" Or are you of all Kings afraid ?
  " For once, good RENARD, in reply
" Be frank, be candid, as am I,
" For I confefs—I am not fick ;
" Nor have been: it was all a trick,
" I fpread abroad the falfe report,
" T' inveigle fimpletons to Court.
" From every part in crouds they came :
" I afk'd their help, my Will to frame;
" They gave it; putting in a claim
" To fomething, each ;—a Mourning Ring ;—
" A Coin ;—a Medal :—any thing :—
" Not for the value they would take,
" But keep it merely for my fake.
  " They little thought *how* I 'd fulfil
" The hidden purpofe of my Will.
" Only put in your head ; look round :
" Guefs, by thefe bones that ftrew the ground,
" What fort of legacies they found.
  " Now, tell me, RENARD, how it happ'd,
" You were not, like the reft, entrapp'd ?"

  ' Sire, (fays the Fox,) my maxim is,—
' (Your pardon if I fpeak amifs,)
' No MONARCH ABSOLUTE TO TRUST,
' However clement, good, and juft.

                    ' But

'But when—(I pardon aſk again—)
'We 've One, who during a ſhort reign
'Whole hecatombs of Beaſts has ſlain;
'Without the leaſt pretext, or cauſe;—
'Juſtice againſt,—againſt all Laws;———
'But what is Juſtice? What are Laws,
'In FRANCE, oppoſed to LEO's paws?'—

"Spare your philippic :—to the point."

'*The times,* I ſay, *are out of joint.*' *—

The LION chafed, and ſhook his mane:
"What! you 're remonſtrating again?"

'Then, thus :—no ſooner had I heard
'The royal ſummons than I fear'd
'Some ſtratagem,—ſome foul-play meant.
'And whilſt the credulous were bent
'On paying homage, alias court,
'I thought I 'd wait ſome friend's·report.

'I might have waited long, indeed;
'For in the footſteps to your Den,
'How many Beaſts went *in*, I read;—
'But not one foot ſtepp'd *out* again.'

* S H A K S P.

N   *FABLE*

F A B L E   XXX.

The FOWLER *and the* HAWK.

A FOWLER obferving a Pigeon one day
Purfued by a HAWK, and near falling its prey;
Uplifted his gun, and his aim took fo well,
The Pigeon efcaped, and the HAWK wounded fell.
Obferving, however, fome fymptoms of life,
The FOWLER drew out of his pocket a knife
To finifh it quite.   At the inftant the ftroke
Impended, the Bird thus the FOWLER befpoke.
' Why, furely, you will not fo barbarous be,
' Without provocation to murder poor me!
' What harm have I done you? Have I ever ftole
' A Pigeon from you? No; not one by my foul.
' If caught in your garden, or yard I had been ;—
' Or hovering over your Pigeon-houfe feen;
' Then might you have kill'd me.   Had that been the
                                                      [cafe,
' I 'd not have afk'd quarter;—expected no grace.
' But, as matters are, I infift you enlarge
' Me; or lay i'you can fome offence to my charge.'

                                        " Give

" Give over your prating: (The FOWLER replies.)
" I 've mark'd your mifdeed,—have I not?—with thefe
[eyes.
" A Pigeon you feized on ; and would have imbrued,
" If I had not ftopp'd you, your talons in blood.
" The mifchief you meant to another to do,
" As juftice demands, fhall be meted to you."

Uplifting his hand and the knife, as he faid;
Without further parley he cut off its head.

FABLE

F A B L E   XXXI.

The BEAR on his Travels.

SOME Poultry drinking at a brook,
    As ufual, at each fip they took
Their heads they lifted up on high ;
And feem'd to gaze upon the fky.

  As they were doing fo, a BEAR,
From Norway, or—no matter where,—
Obferving them, put up his paws
In wonder: and demands ' the caufe
' Of doing fo ?'

            A COCK, endued
With fenfe, replies—" From gratitude.
" I never yet or eat, or drank,—
" Nor will,—without returning thank
" To him, the gracious Deity,
" Who doth our daily wants fupply."

  The BEAR, without religion bred,
Scoff'd at his gratitude ; and faid :—
' Well; in my life I never heard
' Of any cuftom fo abfurd !
' Thank JUPITER each time you quaff !—
' By all the Gods, you make me laugh.'

T he

The Cock indignantly replies,
(Refentment flafhing from his eyes,)
" I know not in what Country you
" Were born; nor where you 're going to.—
" From deferts, not unlike, broke loofe:
" Yet not ev'n that were an excufe
" For your behaviour. Though of Reading
" Ignorant;—and void of Breeding:—
" Though from an. unenlighten'd Nation ;—
" Without inftruɛtion, education ;—
" Simply from reafon might you know,—
" Almoft from inftinɛt, what you owe
" Of reverence to Him who feeds
" Us all, and furnifhes our needs.
  " But, were it no religious rite,—
" Only a cuftom ;—fure you might,
" Whilft with us, pay a deference
" To local modes: not give offence.
  " Why take fuch pains to prove you are
" A downright, worthlefs, fenfelefs *BEAR?*"

F A B L E XXXII.

The FROGS *desiring a King.*

A Commonwealth of FROGS long happy lived,
Free, in their marshes; and grew fat, and thrived:
In this one thing particularly blest,
That no one Frog could lord it o'er the rest.
Ah! happy people!—had they known to prize *
Their envied Freedom, high Immunities!
  By some fatuity they wish'd to vie
With other States, in regal dignity:
And would into a Monarchy erect
Their own; in order to command respect.
But sensible, withal, no one of them
Was fit to wear the royal Diadem.
If honour'd with it, pride would so inflate
That Frog; and so much jealousy create
In others; it might overturn the State.
Rather than risk so much, they wish'd to have
A Foreigner, though e'er so great a Knave.

  To JOVE they offer up a pray'r,—"" that He
""" On some one would confer the Dignity.""

  JOVE heard their pray'r; and in a merry mood,
Sent them a harmless King,—*a Log of Wood.*

* *O, fortunatos nimium, sua si bona norint!*

As

As from Olympus' towring height it fell
Into the marfh, the noife was terrible.
Quickly its Subjeĉts panic-ftruck retire
Amongft the Reeds, or dive into the Mire.
The ftouteft hearts amongft them were afraid;
But the old Quidnuncs were the moft difmay'd:
They fhook their heads, reproaching one another:—
' 'Tis, as I faid 't would be: ay, Brother, Brother;
' This curft ambition you 'll have caufe to rue.
' O! madnefs! What had we with Kings to do?
' Look to your heads. Methinks I hear the axes
' Already whetting for us. Death and Taxes!—
' Shall we not, think ye, have a yearly Budget?
' Or *Water-Tax*. 'Tis now too late to grudge it.
' I tremble, too, for what we more muft bear,
' If a mad Minifter fhould go to war.
' Then,—the King's houfehold. How will ye fupport
' That monfter? Will ye ftarve to feed the Court?

Water-Tax.] Alluding perhaps, by parody, to the *LAND-TAX*
of Great-Britain; an unwife, unjuft, unequal, and oppreffive Tax:
particularly oppreffive now; becaufe, although the War ended four
years fince, the Tax is ftill levied at the rack Rate.

It is not to vex our Minifter, PITT, (for of him I have fo high
an opinion, that I believe the Salvation of this Country depends
upon his continuance in office;)—nor can it be fuppofed to be for my
own particular intereft, I fpeak:—an *Author* and a *Landholder*—
(though fome of us write ourfelves *Efquires*)—are very diftinĉt terms.
I do but note this in order to call the attention of Mr. PITT, (or the
Minifter for the time being,) to the fubjeĉt; and to prepare the minds
of interefted perfons to expeĉt an alteration in the mode of levying the
Land-Tax; for, fooner or later, under certain modifications, it muft
take place.

For,

' For, if his Queen, and Tadpole progeny
' Should of the fame enormous ftature be,
' Few meals our aqueous diftricts will fupply :
' Soon, very foon they 'll drink our marfhes dry.'

Thus forry were they JOVE had heard their pray'r;
And would the whole had been difperfed in air.

The King, however, lay fo long afleep,
Or dead, the FROGS refolved to take a peep.
Nearer, and nearer, by degrees they drew;
And of his *facred perfon* got full view.
On every fide of him whole hours they fwim;
And gaze; but know not what to make of him,
   After much reconnoitering, a Frog
Renown'd for valiance leap'd upon King Log.
Encouraged by his boldnefs others try,
By gentle jogs, to roufe his Majefty:
They pinch, and pufh; and various ways effay;
In vain: inert, and motionlefs he lay.
Which made them doubt, if really it were
A King; and whether JOVE had play'd them fair.
   A learn'd Ontologift who came to fee,
Amongft the reft, this fign of Royalty,
Afferted roundly,—" It was not endued
" With life: no organs had: nor flefh; nor blood. }
" A mere unanimated piece of Wood.
" And,—they might take his word,—a lifelefs thing
" Would never make an active, buftling King."

                                        Since

Since of their Log they could not entertain
Great hopes, they pray'd to JUPITER again.
""" 'Trufting, this time he would not with them fport;
""" But fend a Monarch of *fome other fort.*"

JOVE heard their fecond mad requeft; and fent
Forthwith a *Stork:* by way of punifhment.

A *different* Monarch, truly, proved the *Stork:*
With his long beak he quickly fell to work.
The FROGS his fury and his hunger feel:
For hundreds fcarcely furnifh out a meal.
No Citizen at Greenwich ever eat
More Fry, or White-bait at an annual Treat:
Though he had ftarved himfelf two days before,
That he might gormandize fo much the more.

To JOVE once more the FROGS prefer a pray'r:
""" Humbly entreating him their lives to fpare:—
""" Withdraw the *Stork:* for till he is withdrawn,
""" Nor can the males make love, nor females fpawn,
""" In fafety. Soon of Frogs will be an end,
""" Unlefs fome Stork-killer fhould ftand their friend.
""" For, can they think of Miftreffes or Wives,
""" Who are not fure one minute of their lives?'"

JOVE knit his brows; and angrily replied,—
' Ye have brought on your ruin, by your pride.
' The happieft Nation in the world ye were:
' Unfhackled, uncontroul'd; no King, no care.

O

' Sated

' Sated with happinefs, Ye needs would be
' Exalted;—rather would be great, than free.
' Inclined to make you quiet, if I cou'd,
' I fent a harmlefs King, a Log of Wood.
·' But ye would not with fuch be fatisfied:
' Ye would an *active one*:—by your *own choice* abide,'

For Nations to be bleft, they muft be free.
Republicans.   Or,—ruled,—their King fhould be
Inert,—and next to a non-entity.
   Too active Spirits jealoufy create.
With iron fceptre Tyrants rule a State.
Their wretched Subjects of their wealth they drain,
Themfelves at home in fplendour to maintain,
Or if to War addicted, much they load
Their People, to acquire a name abroad.

FABLE

F A B L E XXXIII.

The BITCH, and the HIND.

A Fox accuftom'd to divert
    Himfelf with fcribbling poetry,
Without intending it had hurt
A BITCH of his vicinity.

His Satire was not aim'd at her ;
For not till afterwards he knew,
It hit fo well her chara&ter ;
And that fhe was a very Shrew.

Nathlefs She every where abufed
    The Fox.—' Lud ! Madám ;—have you feen
' His verfes ?—Mifs ; have you perufed
    ' His Tale ?—What can the Creature mean ?'

" You need not, fure, (replies a HIND ;)
    " The meaning of the Tale be told :
" Nothing is eafier to find :————
    " The Moral is,—*We mufl not—fcold.*

" 'Tis odious ; and 'tis foolifh, too :
    " Why fhould we ftrain our little lungs ?
" Bland looks, and mild addrefs will do
    " More than a thoufand brazen tongues."

F A B L E

F. A B L E XXXIV.

The HARE, and the FROGS.

A HARE unprincipled of life was tired :
One, who old Roman *cowardice* admired :
That *little* act by the *great* CATO done ;
And not enough reproved by ADDISON.
　The ills of life much more than death he fear'd ;
And fuicide as heroifm he revered.
Nervous his cafe.　At the leaft noife he heard
He ftarted.　When the wind the branches ftirr'd,
They to his agitated fancy feem
Or Men, or Dogs, come in purfuit of him.
' There was no other creature to be found
' So curft; (he faid:) and wifh'd that he were drown'd.'

　Diftraught with fpleen, with fullennefs and pride,
One day he walk'd towards the river's fide,
Intent on death.　Herbs by the way he ate
Of force the fenfes to intoxicate,
And lull the thought of an hereafter ftate.
　Ere now the fool had plung'd him headlong in ;
Ere now his Ghoft in Tartarus had been ;—
Had not fome FROGS, that near the river were,
Scared at that formidable beaft—a HARE,—
Precipitately fled.—' O, ho!—(fays He :)—
' Are there, then, Animals afraid of me?

　　　　　　　　　　　　　　　　　　I 'm

' I 'm of more confequence than erft I thought :
' And will no longer fet my life at nought.
' I will not drown me.   No :—I thank thee, JOVE,
' In name of all our Species, for thy love :—
' Abundant love : in that thou didft not pleafe
' To make us HARES—as timorous as thefe.'

Would impious Man, when ftanding on the brink
Of felf-deftruction, paufe awhile, and think
How many Creatures in the world there be
Worfe off,—more abject,—wretcheder than he :
Inftead of aggravating fancied woes,
He would confefs how *much* to *Providence* he owes.

Every Writer who has told this Fable, from ESOP, the Inventor, down to honeft CROXALL, has told it, as of the whole race of HARES going to drown themfelves : than which nothing can be more ridiculoufly imagined.   We hear now and then of an individual weak and wicked enough to make away with himfelf : but to reprefent a *whole na-tion*,—nay more—a *whole fpecies* as about to do fo, is to burlefque a fubject which requires furely to be treated with great folemnity.

F A B L E

F A B L E XXXV.

The THIEF, *and his* MOTHER.

FOR *young* folks commonly are told
Fables; but this is for the *old*:
For Parents, Guardians, Masters, All
To whose discretion Children fall.

Early correct what 's done amiss;
For Habit Second-Nature is.

INDIGNA had an only CHILD,
Which, as an only one, she spoil'd.
(Pray Madam;—look me in the face;—
Tell me; is this your Urchin's case?
If 'tis, reform him young, ere you
Have cause his fatal end to rue.)
INDIGNA's pleasure was to see
Her TONY's tricks and waggery:
However mischievous, her TONY
Still was her *Jewel,—Joy,—*and *Honey.* *

---

* *Jewel*—is a cant name of endearment all over England; *Joy*—
is peculiar to the North; and *Honey* to Ireland. As there are foolish
Mothers, and roguish Boys of every district, the Reader is at liberty to
apply the Story wherever he thinks proper.

No

No wonder every day he did
Mifchief: for never being chid,
How fhould he good from evil learn?—
How the right way from wrong difcern?
By Nature's fimple guidance?———No:
To *Education* 'tis we owe
Our moral excellence. It lies
In that, to make us good and wife.
'Tis *Difcipline* muft exorcife
The dev'lifh paffions which within
Us domineer. The feeds of Sin,
If fuffered deeply to take root,
Will fcarcely e'er be gotten out.

As Man, as well as Beafts, delights
In gratifying appetites,
Gluttons, and Drunkards all would be,
If Nature got the maftery.

Children (but little Men) will fteal
To furnifh a luxurious meal:
Sometimes for wantonnefs. And lie
Swear, and forfwear, for Property.

As early as you can define
The terms poffeffive " thine," and " mine."

To

To which diftinctions *civil* add
Knowledge of what is good and bad
In *morals:* with which intermix
Religion. You'll be fure to fix
His principles: and you may truft
Him fafely: he will e'er be juft.

Not fo her Son INDIGNA taught:
With no fuch leffons was he fraught.
TONY was left at large, to play
His precious infant hours away,
Without correction, or controul.
He was not fent, till late, to fchool:
And when he was, INDIGNA's pray'r
Was,—"" from the cruel birch to fpare
"" Her darling, only Son, and Heir.""
Such ftore fhe fet by this her jewel:
And kind was,—only to be cruel. *
TONY, by habit idle, took
To mifchief, more than to his book.
And being from correction free
Practifed all kinds of roguery.
For parts he had; and might have vied
In good; but being mifapplied,
He eminently bad became:
And grew into opprobrious fame.

* *I muft be cruel, only to be kind.* SHAKSP.

By his addrefs he cheated Boys
Both of their money, and their toys.
And, befide what he won at play,
He pilfer'd fomething every day;
Which cunningly he carried home.
INDIGNA, joy'd to fee him come,
Inftead of whipping him, or other
Punifhment grave, this foolifh Mother
Was wont her TONY to carefs,
And praife him for his clevernefs.
  At length he got to fuch a pafs
Of wickednefs, expell'd he was   }
From School. And now—too late alas!—
INDIGNA grieved fhe had not done
Her duty better by her Son.
In vain fhe now began to preach.
Nothing was fafe within his reach.
So thoroughly adept was he
In flight-of-hand, and thievery,
He ftole—(which one could fcarce fuppofe)—
Her fpectacles from off her nofe,

Though TONY's dexterity may fuffer by a comparifon with MER-
CURY's, I cannot refift the pleafure of tranfcribing a Stanza from the
great Lyric Bard; which if it did not furnifh me the idea, immediately
after occurred.

    Te, boves olim nifi reddidiffes
    Per dolum amotas, puerum minaci
    Voce dum terret, viduus pharetra
        Rifit Apollo.

P   Whilft

Whilſt ſhe a draw'r was looking o'er
For ſomething he had ſtol'n before.

His Boyhood badly gotten through,
Much was ſhe puzzled what to do
With TONY come to man's eſtate:
And dreaded what might be his fate.
Too true her apprehenſions bode:
He took, at twenty, to *the Road.*
Robbery, which he early made
His praɛtice, now became his Trade.—
Moſt perilous, precarious one!
Ere many months his courſe was run.
Deteɛted in a Robbery,
Taken, and tried: condemn'd to die.

Before the fatal cord was tied
He begg'd to ſpeak a word aſide
Unto his weeping Mother; who
Had come to take a laſt adieu.

INDIGNA drew her TONY near;
And putting cloſe her head to hear;
He ſuddenly bit off her ear.

The Standers-by a deep groan fetch,
Shock'd at ſo barbarous a wretch:
And with one general voice they ſaid,—
"" Hang him:—'tis fit that he were dead.""

The Felon penitently bow'd :
Then thus befpoke the angry Crowd.
‘ I wonder not, Spectators, you
‘ Are fhock'd at what you 've feen me do.
‘ Moft ftrange it muft appear that I,
‘ *Launching into eternity,*
‘ By fuch a crime fhould aggravate
‘ Punition in my after-ftate.
‘ But know,—this Woman, which you fee,
‘ This *Mother* 't was, that ruin'd me.
‘ Had I, when early I tranfgrefs'd,
‘ Been flagellated ;—not carefs'd :—
‘ Had I been punifh'd, as I ought,
‘ I had not to this end been brought.'

FABLE

F A B L E   XXXVI.

The MONKEY *and the* HORSE.

A Rider, alias Traveller,
 MONKEY yclept the Beaſts among,
Would fain ſet up a character
 For humour, merriment, and ſong.

Into whatever place he came
 Antics he play'd; affected fun.
And if he thought a Creature tame,
 Him he was ſure to play upon.

At Aſſes, and at Mules expence
 The laugh ſo often had he raiſed,
He ventured once to give offence
 To a brave HORSE which near him grazed.

The HORSE with patience heard him out,
 But when the fool grinn'd ſelf-applauſe,
Laſh'd out indignantly his foot,
 And broke the ſaucy MONKEY's jaws.

Would every one his vengeance wreak
 On ſuch pert fools, it were no matter.
Who cannot to good purpoſe ſpeak,
 Had better not attempt to chatter.

F A B L E

F A B L E   XXXVII.

The MAN, and the TIPULA.

A Group of Gnats a MAN moleft,
A TIPULA amongft the reft.
The MAN in anger fwoop'd his hand ;—
(Boys who catch flies will underftand :)
The TIPULA alone was ta'en ;
And juft when going to be flain,
For mercy thus the MAN addreft :
' I never hurt you ; I proteft.
' Search for my fting : examine me.
' As Naturalift—you 'll find, that we
' TIPULAS, though in body, wings,
' And legs, like Gnats,—yet have no ftings.'

" It may be fo ; (the MAN replies :)
" But though by thefe my proper eyes
" Convinced, you ne'erthelefs fhould die—
" For keeping fuch bad company."

FABLE

F A B L E · XXXVIII.

The Boy, and the Goldfinch.

OUT of its Cage a GOLDFINCH by good luck
Efcaped; and to a neighbouring thicket took
Its flight.— 'T was follow'd by its little MASTER
With aching eyes; lamenting his difafter.
As 't was impoffible the Bird to reach,
The cunning Rogue attempted by fair fpeech
To win upon the GOLDFINCH; and engage
The Rover to return to his old Cage.
'Mongft other things the artful Youngfter faid;—
' You little think how poorly you 'll be fed.
' Not as with me, fupplied with fineft feed;
' And every thing of which you ftood in need.
   ' How can you, GOLDY, wifh abroad to range?
' All things about you muft appear moft ftrange.
' Accuftom'd to a calm, domeftic life,
' How will you brook the buftle, noife, and ftrife
' Which you will meet with? Enemies you 'll find
' Numberlefs; not except your proper kind.
' You as an Interloper they will treat,—
' A Stranger Gueft, come to devour their meat.
' Ere fettled in a comfortable home
' Mifchances many may upon you come.

                                        ' Return,

' Return, then, GOLDY ; and as heretofore
'. I 'll love you ; or—if poffible—yet more.'

“ I thank you (fays the GOLDFINCH) for your love.
“ 'Tis not from that I 'm anxious to remove,
“ But from the *Cage.* Reftraint does not agree ⎫
“ With noble Spirits. I would needs be free. ⎬
“ Come what, come may,—*I 've got my liberty.*” ⎭

Which faid, directly out of fight he flew;
Still chirping, as he went;—“ 1 'm *free* :—adieu;
. [adieu.”

Come what, come may.] SHAKSP.

FABLE

F A B L E   XXXIX.

WISDOM's *Dictate.*

AS FORTUNE with her Child one day
Airing, met PALLAS in her way;
' Dear Sifter, be fo kind (fays fhe)
' With your advice to favour me.
 ' This Child of mine is beautiful ;
' And amiable ;—yet far from dull.
' Her dow'r will be immenfe, you know.
' Now tell me, PALLAS, what to do,
' Not only to prevent diftrefs,—
' But to enfure her happinefs.'

WISDOM, who could not err, replied,—
" Let her have VIRTUE for her Guide."

FABLE

F A B L E   XL.

The L A P - D O G, and. the A s s.

OUR talents we muſt nicely weigh,
    Would we be fafe from ridicule.
Blockheads ſhould not affe⁣ct to play
With Wit; it is a ſharp-edged tool.

A Countryman a LAP-DOG kept;
A favourite one, that play'd, ate, flept
The Children with : whate'er their fun
TYCHO was fure of making one.
Though he pleafed every body, yet,
None liked him half fo well as BET.
She took the trouble once a week
To waſh him clean, and comb him fleck.
Near her, or on her knees he fat
At meals; and niceſt morfels ate
Out of her hand, or off her plate.

A jealous JACK-ASS, who perceived
How favour went, was greatly grieved.
And thus was overheard one day
In deep foliloquy to bray :——

' Say, great LEUCIPPUS, EPICURUS,
' Ye-learn'd Men-Affes, who affure us
' That every thing was made by Chance,
' Say, in the Atoms firft grand Dance,
' Was it not, think ye, very hard
' That my Progenitor was marr'd
' In making? Had it come to pafs,
' Inftead of being a mere Afs,
' His atomies had clang together
' In fhape of Horfe,—or Lap-Dog rather,
' Then I, like TYCHO had been blefs'd;
' Made much of, fondled, and carefs'd.
    ' See how the envied Creature ftands
' Neftling its head in BETSY's hands!
    ' Why makes fhe about him this fufs?
' What is the diff'rence betwixt us?
' Is it becaufe the little Wretch
' Can fit-an-end;—and fawn;—and fetch
' And carry;—and jump over fticks;—
' And other fuch like eafy tricks?
' I warrant I could do as much,
' If I'd defcend to trifles fuch.
    ' This very afternoon will I,—
' Yes, I'm refolved upon 't, I'll try.
' Firft,—I muft learn *to give the pat*:—
' There's nothing difficult in that.
' At fuppertime I'll take my place
' By BAUCIS; and I'll ftroke her face;

                                    ' And

' And pat her Cheeks ; and fteal a kifs ;—
' No ;—not of Madam ;—but, of Mifs :
' I'll kifs the Daughter : any other,—
' Ball, if he will, may kifs the Mother.'

Though you may think the Ass·abfurd,
Or joking ; faith, he kept his word.
Into the Hall he hies to fup ;
And fits him down upon his croup,
Clofe by the lovely Betsy's fide :
And looks about with no lefs pride
Than an intruding Burgher, who
A vifit makes Sir Bribewell to ;
And being prefs'd to ftay and dine
Is feated by My Lady fine.
The only difference is this,—
One is not afk'd, the other is.

When Tycho faw the Ass approach
His Miftrefs, near enough to touch
Almoft, he bark'd ; as well he might :
And fhow'd his teeth,—but durft not bite.
    The Family are in a pother :
The Children bawl one to another.
" Why ! look ye, now, at yonder Bee-aft !—
" He 's come to keep our Whitfon Fee-aft."

Susan, the fimple Servant Maid,
At the ftrange fight was much afraid.

                                    Starting

Starting afide, fhe tumbled o'er
A ftool; and fprawl'd upon the floor.
There trembling, panting as fhe lay,
Thus fervently began to pray.
' Great JOVE avert from us all evil.
' Save from this four-legg'd afs-like Devil
' Me, wicked Wretch: I'll never fin
' Again:—do nought but few, and fpin.
' Come FRANK, come THOMAS, when they may,
' I'll *vartuous* be; and fay 'em " Nay."
' Not ev'n my favourite, Valet HARRY,
' Shall kifs me more,—unlefs he'll marry.
    ' Save me from this foul fiend.'——She faid;
And in her apron hid her head.

    BAUCIS, though now a Farmer's Wife,
Had in the former part of life
Been in a Lady's fervice; where
The home-taught, hopeful Son and Heir
By Pedagogus every matin
Was coax'd to read a page of Latin:
By often hearing OVID read,
Or talk'd of, took it in her head
That all the fimple Tales he told
Had truly happ'd in days of old.
In fhort, the learned Farmerefs
Believed in Metamorphofes.

                                        She

She fpies the Ass; and thinks it odd is;
Yet ftill has hope that it fome God is :-—
" Who knows but fornicating Jove,
" Who once turn'd Bull-calf to make love,
" And carried off Europa, may
" Intend fome amorous prank to play
" With Betsy?—And in truth, my Daughter
" May make e'en Jupiter's Mouth water."

So argued Baucis: but her Hub,
Plain Man, began his head to fcrub.
Of Ovid's tales he nothing knew;
Nor what his Wife alluded to.
Scarcely could he forbear from laughter,
To think a God fhould like his Daughter:
Howe'er, not coveting the honour
Of feeing Jupiter upon her;
Behind the Ass he took his ftand
With oaken cudgel in his hand;
And juft as Jack his paw uprears,
Gave him a ftroke betwixt the ears:
Another;—and another;—till
Jack, finding he was ufed fo ill,
Set up a loud and hideous bray,
That ftunn'd them all: and ran away.

F A B L E

FABLE XLI.

The ANTELOPE, and the STAG.

AN ANTELOPE, who got a wound,
  Himself fequefter'd from the herd;
And dying, by a STAG was found,
Who thus put in a well-meant word.

'It hurts me much, my friend, to hear
  'Of your mifhap, but more to fee
'You thus; with no acquaintance near,
  'Nor any of your family.

'Permit me, Sir, to fend your Wife,
  'Your Children to you;—and your Friends:
'Although they can not fave your life;—
  'Kindnefs to confolation tends.''

" How little (fays the ANTELOPE)
  " Know you of true philofophy!
" I 'd fend, if I of life had hope;—
  " But not to let them fee me die.

" My wound, long fince I underftood,
  " Nor cure admits of, nor relief:
" Since, then, my Friends can do no good,—
  " Wherefore fhould they partake my grief?''

FABLE

F A B L E XLII.

The BOY, and the BUTTERFLY.

A Truant SCHOOLBOY rambling in a field,
A BUTTERFLY moft beautiful beheld,
And gave it chace : from flow'r to flow'r it flew ;
Out of his reach, but ftill within his view.
The BOY, with pertinacity endued,
Faft as it fled, as eagerly purfued ;
Until the BUTTERFLY, fatigued at length,
Settled upon a flow'r without the ftrength
To rife again. The BOY, for fear it fhou'd,
Sprang at the FLY as nimbly as he cou'd :
But, with fo violent a grafp he feized,
Marr'd the fine colours which his eye had pleafed.
That now, inftead of giving him delight,
The BUTTERFLY was hateful to his fight.
The verieft Reptile that e'er crawl'd the earth
Seem'd now of equal, or fuperior worth.

The moral of this Fable I deduce,—
(Left you miftake it,)—Reader, for your ufe.
You are the BOY : your *fcheme of happinefs*
A FLY—by allegory we exprefs.

Picafure

Pleasure 's the Object we have all in view,—
The gewgaw Insect which we all pursue.
And if we rudely seize it, we destroy
Our blifs ; ourselves annihilate our joy.

Let us not be too eager in the chace ;—
The Object not too ardently embrace.
By these, and only by these means we may
Protract our Pleasures to our latest day.

F A B L E

F A B L E XLIII.

The LEARNED-DOG, *and the* DUNCE.

A Boy of parts, and yet a DUNCE——
 ' *How can that be ?—What both at once ?* '

Why not ?—Parts are but faculties
Which dormant left, leave men unwife.
Parts are no more than latent worth
Which *Education* muft call forth.

  ' *In what confifteth Education ?—*
' *Muft we by Terrour, Emulation,*
' *Or Hope :—by which, or all combined,*
' *Affect we moft the infant mind ?* '

With diff'rent Children diff'rent ways
(Defpite of what HELVETIUS fays)
Muft be purfued.   The *temper* ftrike :
No two are organized alike.
This Boy the Rod alone regards ;
That is excited by Rewards.
  But 'tis my prefent Fable's aim
To fhow, that nothing works like *SHAME.*

  ROBERT——or BOB, for fhortnefs, we
Will call him,—had capacity ;

R

Yet

Yet, by fome unaccountable
Perverfenefs, could not read, nor fpell,
Not ev'n his name at fix years old.
'T was not for want of being told
Often enough; for never Lad
More worthy, anxious Parents had:
The Mother in particular.
The tafk of teaching fell to her.
For Children's tender years demand
Indulgence more than reprimand.
And Women hold a tighter rein
Over their tempers than we Men:—
As far as *Teaching* goes.—I wou'd
Not boundlefsly be underftood.

  Infinite pains PERDIGNA took
To make her Urchin mind his book.
She begg'd, or bribed him every day
To try his Alphabet to fay.
Frequently brought him frefh fupplies
Of gilded Books from NEWBERY's.
The Pictures BOB examined well;
But not a letter would he tell.
The Bodkin, twofold Implement,
Oft in the bootlefs fervice bent.

  You, Reader *gentle*,—if you be,
And blefs'd with fenfibility
To relifh a domeftic fcence,—
May have obferved,—and have, I ween,—

                                        An

An interefting little Print,—
(Etching perhaps, or Metzotint, *)
" THE PRUDENT MOTHER " call'd ; in which
A Matron anxious feems to teach
A Boy his Letters. But while She
Is pointing with her Bodkin, He
Turns his arch eyes another way ;
Refolved his leffon not to fay :
And, that he may not even hear,
He ftops perverfely either ear.

* *Mezzotinto.*] It is very well the Rhime obliged me to cut off
the *o* final ; as, by fo doing, and changing the firft *z* into a *t*, I have
preferved as much as need be of the Italian Sound ; and at the fame
time have *anglicifed* the word : as ought to be all foreign words which
it is found expedient to adopt.

Rich as our Language already is, I am very far from wifhing not
to enrich it yet more by the acquifition of foreign Words, be they
Italian, French, Latin, or Greek, or from whatever fource they be ;
quocunque de fonte cadunt ;—fi parce diftorta :—that is,—upon condition they be fuited to our pronunciation, and orthography. But I
enter my formal proteft againft the adoption of frivolous French Words,
accentuated to be fpoken as they are at PARIS. It becomes the dignity of JOHN BULL to reject them at all times, but more efpecially
in folemn difcourfe, or in Books of Science.

Who would have expected to meet with the word *opiniâtretè* in the
very elegant and fcientific Work of a Profeffor of one of our Uni-
verfities ?—

If the learned Prelate, to whofe Work I allude, fhould perchance fee
this my curfory animadverfion, he will not, I hope, attribute it to any
want of refpect in me. No one is a greater admirer of his Lordfhip's
literary talents ;—his erudition, his fcience, his manlinefs, and libe-
rality of fentiments.—It was the excellency, indeed, of his Writings,
that attracted my critical obfervation. Had his language in general
been lefs highly polifhed, fo flight a flaw would not have been dif-
cernible. It is a faint fpot upon the Sun's difk ; which in a lefs lu-
minous Orb had not been vifible.

Our.

Our little Bob was fuch another
Urchin; and harrafs'd fo his Mother.
What prudence dictated, fhe did;
Sometimes fhe coax'd him, fomteimes chid:
Without effect. The Father lent
His aid: inflicted punifhment
Corporal : and confined him too:
Of play abridged him. Nought would do.

Sure, never worthy Parents were
Plagued with a more unworthy Heir.

By chance into their country came
A Dog of literary fame :
Who,—befides cuftomary tricks,
Jumping through hoops, and over fticks,—
Could fpell a name; and pick out letters,
Better than many of his Betters.

Shock's wonderous qualities, and worth
Were in a Hand-Bill blazon'd forth.
All which his Mafter, Signor Presto,
Himfelf a Conj'rer, gave atteft to.
' INVITING all the Neighbourhood;—
' Not gratis, be it underflood;—
' For, every one, by juft gradation,
' Is tax'd according to his ftation.

' To

‘ *To* private Audiences SHOCK *goes*,
‘ *And lectures* KINGS—under the *ROSE.* *
‘ DUKES-ROYAL (Hiftory, alafs !
Shows us, what looks like Gold, is Brafs,
Oft times: I mean, that DUKES there are,
Or have been, who beftow’d lefs care
Upon the Mufes, than the Fair.
Love-letters pafs’d; and all was well:
They fcribbled, though they could not fpell.†)
‘ *If there be fuch unlettered* NINNY-
‘ HIGHNESSES *now, pay—HALF-A-GUINEA.*
‘ MARQUISES, EARLS, and VISCOUNTS, *down*
‘ *To Irifh* BARONS, *pay a—CROWN.*
‘ PEERESSES, LADIES, BARONETS,
‘ *And fimple* KNIGHTS, and BANNERETS,
‘ *At—TWO-AND-SIXPENCE.* L. L. D.’s
‘ *And* F. R. S.’s—*WHAT THEY PLEASE.*
‘ *As Literati Brothers, they*
‘ *Are welcome, though they fhould not pay.*

---

* SIGNOR PRESTO meant to pun, no doubt; the ‘ *Rofe* ’ not
ftanding only as part of a Cant Phrafe, but for an ancient Gold
Coin, value about fixteen fhillings.

† *Quere,*—Were not certain Letters to a certain LADY ill-fpelt on
purpofe? Was it not Ignorance *put on,* together with the Black Wig,
by way of difguife? For his HIGHNESS’s Credit we will fuppofe fo.

All

' *All lower Ranks of Perfons willing*
' *To hear the Lecture, pay a—SHILLING*;
' CHILDREN *except: whom* SHOCK *will teach,*
' *(In lap, or not,) at—SIX-PENCE each.*
' *With* Nota Bene, BOYS *who skipp'd*
' *This Leffon, would be furely whipp'd.*
' *Punition worfe for* GIRLS *who mifs'd,*
' *For they were never to be kifs'd.*

  ' *The Doors to ope at Six o'Clock:*
' *So*—VIVANT REX, ET DOCTOR SHOCK.'

BOB's Father, humouring the joke,
Much of SHOCK's parts, and learning fpoke.
' How happy muft his Parents be,
' To have fo learn'd a Whelp as He!
' I fear our two-legg'd Cur will never,
' With all our pains, be half as clever.
' A DOG turn'd Schoolmafter! My Dear.'

  " Wonderful!—BOBBY, do you hear,
" And blufh not?—You, who do not know
" Yet how to fay your Chris-crofs-Row."

  Archly enough the Boy replies;
''' I know, Mamma, I am not wife:
''' But, yet, I am not fuch a fool
''' To think a DOG can keep a School.'''

Pleafed

Pleafed with his *naivety* * they fmiled;
But ftill would fain perfuade the Child
It was fo. If he doubted it,
They challenged him to fet his wit
Againft the Dog's : that is, to try
Which read the better, by and by :
For, if he durft engage him, they
Would go to Shock that very day.
A fair propofal. Bob agreed :
For though he knew he could not read .
Himfelf,—doubting the Stories told
Of Shock,—and naturally bold,—
He was refolved the Dog to meet :
Nor fear'd, nor thought of a defeat.

The Parties all fet of in glee
The learned Animal to fee.

Arrived ; the Father tips the wink
To Presto.—To what end d' ye think ?
—' To notice Bob ; and tafk him.'—Good.
Presto the fignal underftood.

* *Naivety*.] The French word *Naïveté* is creeping into ufe with us ;
and as a word of great delicacy and force, (denoting fomething more than
Simplicity,) it is well worthy adoption :—but, not *as a French word*.
It is very abfurd in us, to fpeak it, and fpell it fo accentuated : particularly as to its final *e* ; which is fo oppofite to the genius of the Englifh Language, that it can never, in that ftate, be naturalized. I have,
therefore, flightly varied its fpelling. A rule I have prefcribed to myfelf for *anglicifing* all foreign words not confo mable to Englifh pronunciation. Which rule, if the Public Critics (*Quos penes arbitrium
eft, et jus et norma loquendi*) think well of it, I hope, they will
pafs it into Law.

Alphabets

Alphabets ranged upon the ground:
Shock was call'd in; and looking round
The crouded Room, refpectfully
Bow'd thrice to all the Company.
  Whether by finger, foot, or what,
Or how,—to us it matters not,—
But Presto had contrived, no doubt,
Some how to fingle Robert out:
For up to him directly goes
The Dog, and takes him by his cloaths;
Nor will return, nor from him ftir:
Which Presto, his interpreter,
Said,—' Was the only way he had
' Of making known what clever Lad
' He wifh'd to cope with: and if He,—
' Master,—before that Company
' Durft prove his fcholarfhip, Shock wou'd
' The fame; and beat him, if he cou'd.'

  Bob blufh'd; and down his eyes he caft:
But recollecting he had paft
His word: he told the man he wou'd:
'" And let Shock beat him,—if he cou'd."'

  ' Pleafe, little Sir, to come this way.
' Shock will come, too; I dare to fay.'

  Together lovingly they come
Into the middle of the Room.
                                   ' Firft

' Firſt, pretty Maſter, what's your name?'
"" Bob.""

  ' Know you how to ſpell the fame?'
The Urchin gave the man a jog:
"" Nay, aſk that queſtion of your Dog.""

 ' He 'll tell it me; and what's more odd,
' Will tell you how to ſpell a *Rod*.
' Shock!—you 've the converſation heard;
' And Maſter's Name: come, ſpell the word.
' If you one letter miſs, you know
' Who fupperleſs to bed will go.—
' Bob is an eaſy name to ſpell:—
' Begin:—take heed: and do it well.'

The Dog walks thrice the letters round
Ranged in two circles on the ground.
Then 'twixt his teeth takes up a "" B;""
And ſhews it to the Company.
"" O,"" next:— and then another "" B.""
Which they with admiration fee.
" Bravo!" they cry; and clap their hands:
All except Bob. Confuſed he ſtands:
Now bluſhing; and now pale, by turns:
His breaſt with indignation burns;
And ſhame commix'd: their pládudits feem
Intended raillery on him.

   S   His

His fpirit can not brook difgrace;
So, he refolves to quit the place.
 His Father fain would have him ftay;
But Bob will not: he hies away,
Faft as he can. And when at home;
Hurried directly to his room,
And fullenly flung into bed;
Without acquainting Man or Maid
Of his arrival: there he lay,
Brooding o'er what had happ'd that day.

 Bob's Parents, inly pleafed to find
That Shame was working in his mind,
Thought better not to interrupt
His mufings: and without him fupp'd.
His Mother only previoufly
Juft peep'd into his Room to fee
That he was fafe: his whim admir'd;
And, without faying ought, retired.

 Shame and vexation fo poffeft
The Infant, that he could not reft:
But reafoning with himfelf he lay:—
  " What will my friends and playmates fay,
  " (Many of whom are not fo old
  " As I am,) when they fhall be told
  " A *Dog* difgraced me?—Envied Shock!
  " Thee they will praife, and me they 'll mock.

" And

AFTER THE MANNER OF LAFONTAINE. 131

"" And is there, then, no way t' efface
"" Remembrance of this dire difgrace ? ·
"" Yes; there 's one way, and only one :—
"" To do as much as SHOCK has done :
"" Or more. Tomorrow I will get
"" By heart,—will *fay* my Alphabet,
"" Which he cannot. At break of day
"" I 'll to it ; and I will not play
"" Till every letter I can fay." -

This refolution form'd, he found
It balfam to his feftering wound.
So good Refolves for ever are :
They foothe the Soul funk down with care ;
And fave it from the fiend—Defpair.

ROBERT at early morn arofe ;
Haftily huddled on his cloaths :
Defcends into the Parlour ; looks
Out one of his own little Books.
The gilded cover back he turns
Indignantly ; the pictures fpurns ;
And ferioufly his Letters learns.

Pleafed were his Parents when they fpied
Their youngfter fo well occupied.
The Father cries ;—' I 'm very glad
' To find you grown a ftudious Lad.'

The

The Mother ;—" Love, why did not you
" Call in as you were ufed to do ?
" You know you fhould not come down ftairs
" Until we 've heard you fay your pray'rs."

"" Forgive me, dear Mamma ; I pray :
"" I 'll not do fo another day.
"" 1 rofe betimes that I might get,
"" Ere you were up, my Alphabet :
"" Which I am perfect in : Will you
"" Hear me ?—And teach me fomething new ?
"" For, I 'm refolved on 't, every day
"" Long leffons as I can to fay.
"" In Learning all my time I 'll pafs :
"" Not be the Blockhead that I was.'"

From that aufpicious hour he took
So great a liking to his book,
A Claffic Scholar he became
Ere long.   O, bleft effect of SHAME !

May I conftruct a ufeful hint on
This Tale, for WESTMONAST : et WINTON :
And other Seminaries, where
Ferules or Rods in ufage are ?
I would not have thofe laid afide
Wholly : but, Shame fhould be applied

As

As an auxiliar.   Youths there are
Who corp'ral punifhment can bear
However fharp ; and glory in
The hardnefs, toughnefs of their *Skin :*
But Ignominy, and Reproach
The moft obdurate *Minds* will touch.

   There 's not a Nation on the earth
Has Men of fuch acknowledged worth,
As England has, for MASTERS ;—would
They but exert them, as they could.
   What pity 'tis that Indolence
Should get the better of Good-fenfe !
They 'd rather tread in the old path
Which many a BUSBY *beaten* hath,
Than ftrike a new one out : their wand,
The *Rod,* is ever in their hand.
   Let GALLIA's Beafts of burden feel,
Slaves as they are, the whip and fteel :
But the free Courfers of our Ifle
Should make a pleafure of their toil.
By Hope, by Emulation they
Should be incited on their way.
If thefe not goad them on to fame,
The proper punifhment is—SHAME.

FABLE

F A B L E   XLIV.

The LION, *and the* THREE BULLS.

WITH longing eye KING LEO watch'd
    Three BULLS that lived in amity.
But, likely to be over match'd,
    His ftrength he durft not with them try.

The BULLS, however, quarrelling
    At laft; no fooner was it known
That they were parted, than the KING
    Fell on, and kill'd them, *one by one.*

If not for love, for fafety fake,
We leagues of amity fhould make;
Which nothing fhould have power to break.

Ουτως ομονοια τοις χρωμενοις σωτηριον. Says APHTHONIUS,
in his dry way.

FABLE

F A B L E XLV.

The COCK *finding a* DIAMOND.

A COCK a-fcratching up the ground
　　In fearch of food, a DIAMOND found,
Which fpurning from him, ' Pfhaw ! (fays he ;)
' A Gem is of no ufe to me.
' Ladies, or Lapidaries might
' In fuch a bawble take delight :—
' Its cut, and colour would admire,
' Perhaps ;—its largenefs, or its fire.
　' To me how welcomer a prize—
● A Barley-corn of half its fize !'

An *Ignoramus* HEIR-AT-LAW,
Rummaging over Papers, faw
A MANUSCRIPT, in crabbed hand,
Of which he did not underftand
A fyllable. " Perhaps, (fays he,)
" This might ineftimable be
" In fome learn'd Antiquary's eyes,
" But how much welcomer a prize
" To me—a Bond, or Banker's Note !
" Foregad ! I would not give a groat
" For all the Manufcripts on Earth.
" Infooth, I wonder of what worth
" The mufty things in the Mufeum !
" Who will may read 'em,—fo I never fee 'em."

F A B L E

F A B L E XLVI.

The CAVALIER, and his HORSE.

A CAVALIER, who had a HORSE that shied
At every thing almost, and sprang aside,
Finding correction was but thrown away,
Thus reason'd with the animal one day.
‘ Why, what a blockhead, coward wretch you are,
‘ To let that harmless thing, a Jack-Ass scare
‘ Such a strong beast! Suppose that he were bent
‘ On an attack,—(by way of argument,)—
‘ Have you not Hoofs to strike with,—Teeth to tear?
‘ Ashame upon you! What have you to fear?’

“ 'Tis very true; the candid HORSE replied:
“ Blockhead I am: it cannot be denied.
“ I blush to think how very terrible
“ Things have appear'd till I have seen 'em well:
“ And then, most readily I ridicule
“ My fears; and inly call myself a Fool.
“ But how much greater fool I 've known *you* be.
“ You start at things you neither hear, nor see;
“ At fancied objects; Phantoms, Ghosts, and Sprites;—
“ Creations of your brain, and murky nights.
“ A truce, good Master: till you grow more wise
“ Yourself, it is not fit you should *philosophize*.”

FABLE

F A B L E XLVII.

The SQUIRE, the MOLE, and the BLACKBIRD.

A GRESTIS in the Country bred
With country notions in his head,—
I mean, fuch notions primitive,
As, how much better 'tis to live
In plenty on one's own eftate
Than out-at-elbows with the Great.
 Wretched the Man, depraved the mind
That cannot in the Country find
Amufement. The Metropolis
Affords but artificial blifs.—
Nay ;—'tis a word's mifufe to call
Intoxication Blifs at all.
 To lofe the firft of bleffings, health,
In wafting,—or acquiring wealth ;
To court ambition ; and to toil
For honours ;—is it worth our while?
To go the rounds of diffipation ;
To fet, or follow every fafhion
That folly can invent ;—is this
What Beings rational call Blifs?

T

To

To live to Luxury: to try
By every means to multiply
Our wants—*but* thofe to gratify;
At whatfoever rifk, expence;
Againft religion, morals, fenfe:
To let vice triumph; and infult
Honour: call poverty a fault,
And riches worth :—————But I 'll not preach.
My Fable's purport is to teach
Men what is Happinefs : to drive
Them from great Cities where they live
In fplendid mifery, and riot,—
To rural fcenes —to blifs and quiet.

    The *Country* far from being dull,
He muft a dullard be and fool
Himfelf that cannot find out ways
Of paffing pleafantly his days.
People of any tafte may bring
Themfelves to fancy Gardening;
Adorning Grounds, or Botany; —
Or honourable Hufbandry.

Honourable Hufbandry.] The unambitious Squire, whofe daily
employ is Agriculture, and who purfues it with the fpirit of a Gentleman,—that is,—with the view of benefiting the Public, rather than
himfelf; making experiments; and communicating improvements, as
he goes along;—how much more worthy is he of the name of *Patriot*,
than the mere Brawler in Parliament;—the Reprefentative of a rotten
Borough, who paffes whole nights in St. STEPHEN's CHAPEL,
for,—*what he is pleafed to call*,—the Good of his Country!

                        Then,

Then, for the paftimes of the Field
Various, which health and vigour yield,—
What are the vantages in Town
Can counterbalance thefe alone?
Can honours, titles, fame, or wealth
Compenfate for the lofs of health?
And, yet, how many, void of fenfe,
In LONDON live, in preference!
There, where PANDORA, and her train
Of evils and difeafes reign.
 AGRESTIS was not of this herd
Of fools; he happily preferr'd ·
His native fields; nor blufh'd to own
He had no relifh for the Town.
Adhering ftrictly to his plan
Of life, as Country Gentleman;
Sollicitous to do what good
He could do in his neighbourhood,
With his advice, or fortune; he
Not doubted of felicity.
But, the firft, greateft good in life,
Is that beft thing,—when good,—a Wife.
Without one, life a void would prove:
'Tis non-exiftence not to love:
Who has a Partner only bleft is:
So faid (who had not tried,) AGRESTIS.

With

With notions liberal like thefe,
The Youth, not rich, but at his eafe,
Look'd round the neighbourhood to find
A Partner fuited to his mind.
It were a pity fhould he meet
With one that would his fchemes defeat.
    He wedded one, who, though fhe brought
No cafh, was rich enough he thought:
For MARIANNE, (that was her name,)
The Parfon's daughter, had the fame
Of being economical;
A quality collateral
With wealth.   Indeed, I 'd rather have
A dow'rlefs Lafs, who knew to fave,
Than one with wealth, without the wit
Of taking proper care of it.
Who to the utmoft of her power
Is frugal, is herfelf a dower.
    MARIANNE befides for houfewifery
With all the Laffes round might vie.
Could net, and few, and puddings make
With any in the wapentake.
    All thefe fhe could, in cafe of need;
But, more accomplifh'd, fhe could read,
And write, converfe, and dance, and fing,
And play; in fhort, do any thing.

                                    Of

Of form and manners elegant;
Admired; beloved; what could fhe want?—
Unlefs it were a Hufband?

                                   ' *Ay:*
' *All Girls, in footh, want that.*'

                              You fay.
I 'll not difpute with you.   They may.
But MARRIANNF, you 'll underftand,
Wanted the beft in all the Land.

' *All would the beft: but ah! how few*
' *Ev'n good ones are entitled to!*'

Hold, Wretch, that too cenforious tongue:
Should you fome Females get among
That I could name, I fancy they
Would make you for your rafhnefs pay.

But, to my Fable.   MARIANNE
Married our Country Gentleman.
Long was their Honey-moon.   He lived
Whole years as if but newly wived.
No kindneffes forgot; nor rites
Omitted: bleft their days and nights.
But one would think 'twas JOVE's decree—
No Couple long fhould happy be
Without encreafe of family.
Though thoufands, and ten thoufands, who
Have Children, the misfortune rue.

                                   Still,

Still, Wives who do not breed,—(and fome
That do,)—are lefs attach'd to home
Than they fhould be. So MARIANNE.
Though far from fool, her fancy ran
Rather too much upon Diverfions;
Races; Affemblies; Balls; Excurfions
To BATH, or BRIGHTON: but the TOWN
Her thoughts were moftly fix'd upon.
' Who had not to Ridottos been,—
' Operas, and Plays;—and never feen
' ST. JAMES's, and the King, and Queen,
' And all their Bairns;—had nothing feen;
' Knew nothing; and had no where been.
  ' She hoped, howe'er, all this that fhe
' Had faid would not miftaken be.
' She was no Rambler, for her part:
' She loved her Hub with all her heart.
  . (AGRESTIS fmiled and thank'd his Spoufe,)
' She doated on the old Hall-Houfe.

ST. JAMES's.] They who *have* feen ST. JAMES's have feen
nothing, or next to nothing in Appearance. It is the fhabbieft Pile of
Buildings that ever great Monarch lived in. The Nation ought for
its own honour, if not for the King's, to erect a new Palace.
The fite fhould be the Centre of HYDE-PARK, or as nearly fo as
might be. It fhould be a Structure to challenge the admiration of
Europe. No matter what time it would take in erecting: fo that it
went gradually on. Let Parliament vote annually Fifty Thoufand
Pounds till it be completed. Such a trifling Sum would not percep-
tibly affect our prefent economic fyftem; and yet would, in twenty
or thirty years, lodge the Monarch for-the-time-being, as the Monarch
of BRITAIN ought to be lodged.

‛ No

' No perfon upon earth could be
' Fonder of rural life than fhe.
' 'T was happinefs fupreme to walk
' Agrestis with, and hear him talk
' Of Hufbandry ; and how much yields
' Each crop ;—how oft he fallows fields ;—
' Manures 'em well : in fhort, fo labours,
' That he furpaffes all his Neighbours.
' O, inexhauftlefs fund of blifs !
' Could a Town life compare with this ?'

" I cannot but admire, my Dear,
" Your fatire, though it is fevere.
" Yours is an inexhauftlefs vein
" Of Irony : go on again."

' The Gardens of th' Hesperides
' Boafted not better bearing Trees.
' Thofe of Alcinous, and Adonis
' Were dull compared with what our own is.
' The artificial Mounts ; and Glens ;
' The Yews cut into Cocks and Hens ;—
' Faunus forefend that any Brown
' *Tafteless* fhould ever cut them down !'

" Who fays that Women are not found
" Worthy to tread on claffic ground ?
" Wife was her Dad to make her pat in
" Mythology ; and teach her Latin.

" Johnson,

" Johnson, the Lexicographer,
" When living was a fool to her.
" In houſehold duties _Blockheads_ might
" Be occupied, and take delight :—
" Pallas be ·praiſed ! his Marianne
" In Wit ſhould cope with any Man ;
" Or ſet of Men : ſhe ſhould engage
" The Literati of the Age."

‘ Far from it. Her ambition went
‘ No higher, than to give content
‘ To him.   The Country ſtill her theme
‘ Humble ſhould be, to pleaſure him.

‘ The caw of Rooks, ſhe could aver,
‘ Was muſic raviſhing to her.
‘ And not a thing about the Farm
‘ She ſaw, or heard, but had its charm.
‘ Was it not pleaſureful to hear
‘ The loud, ſhrill notes of Chanticleer ?
‘ The Ducks, too, quacking in a morning
‘ To give the lazy Wenches warning
‘ When it were time to milk the Kine :—
‘ The low of Oxen :—grunt of Swine :—
‘ The Ploughman talking to his Steers :—
• All theſe were muſic to her ears.

‘ If any thing could give diſguſt
‘ To Country Wives, the Bugle muſt.

                                   ‘ The

' The Huntſman need not wind his horn
' So very early in the morn :
' Tempting her Huſband from her, ere
' She well can ſay—Good morrow, Dear.
' Nor ſeldom carelefs of his health
' And her, he quits his bed by ſtealth.
' Not dreaming that he up and dreſt is,
' She wakes, and ſoftly ſays—AGRESTIS !—
' Raiſes her arm to put it round
' Her Lord, no Lord is to be found.
' Equipp'd, impatient for the chace,
' He cares not for his Wife's embrace :
' The foggy air to warmth prefers ;
' And DIAN's chilly arms to hers.
' Hunting is, ſure, a barb'rous ſport !
' How many Creatures ſuffer for 't.
' But Wives would have lefs cauſe to grieve,
' If Huſbands would take *civil* Leave.' '

" Have you much cauſe to cenſure me,
" As wanting in civility ?"

' Why, no ;—not much :—but men can 't ſhow
' Too much civility, you know.
' Women are better for it : We
' Indulged in every thing ſhould be.

Carelefs of his health, and her.] Manet ſub Jove frigido
Venator, teneræ Conjugis immemor.

U · ' Huſbands

' Hufbands would lead celeftial lives
' Would they be govern'd by their Wives,
' ' In all things ; and at all times grant,
' Without a queftion, what they want.'

" If human nature perfect were,
" And Women too difcreet to err ;—
" Nothing unfit would they. requeft,
" Then all things would be for the beft ;
" And Men in granting would be bleft.
" But tell me, without more ado,
" What this harangue is preface to."

' Not oft I wifh abroad to range ;
' Addicted am I not to change ;
' I 'd not give up my Country life
' To be the PRINCE OF WALES's Wife,
' Were I obliged to live in Town,
' The whole year round ; but I muft own,
' A jaunt there for fix weeks, or fo,
' When RUSTIC HALL is white with fnow,
' Would give me almoft as much joy,
' As having a fine, *chopping Boy*.'

The words ' a chopping boy ' ftill clofed
Her fpeech, whatever fhe propofed.
It was an artifice fhe ufed
In order not to be refufed.

For, fhe a maxim held it, No man
Ought to refufe a childlefs Woman.
As if the fault muft ever be
In him, not her fterility.

AGRESTIS long accuftom'd to
Her gibes, indifferent of them grew.

The fame thing faid too often o'er,
After a while affects no more.
As bells may jar upon the ear
Until one can no longer hear.

What 's to be done, then?—MARIANNE,
I warrant, will devife fome plan
For compaffing her wifhes.—Or
She is not what I took her for.

AGRESTIS, though he would not grant
Her wifh immediate of a Jaunt
Of *Pleafure*, her fo far he loved,
He might by other means be moved:
Should fhe fall *fick*, no doubt he would
Do for her all a Hufband could.
Convinced of this, fhe ficknefs feign'd;
Of head-achs, colds, and coughs complain'd:
Of agues, fevers,—and what not,—
By living in the Country got.

In ASHENFORD, not far from them,
Lived the learn'd Dr. APOZEM.

Sent

Sent for of courfe, the Doctor came,
Blifter'd, and bled, and purged the Dame.
Bred in FOOTE's School, he open'd wide
All doors; by all expedients tried
T' expell the foe.   The Doctor's fkill
Was great: his motto—"" Cure, or kill.""'
In prefent cafe of both he fail'd:
For though the Lady little ail'd,
His phyfic did nor harm, nor good:
But *wherefore* fhould be underftood:
It was her prudence, not her luck,
Saved her: fhe very rarely took
Powders, or Pills: they were convey'd
Away by SUK, her trufty Maid.

 Yet MARIANNE grew worfe, and worfe;—
As fhe pretended :—and, of courfe
Alarm'd AGRESTIS; who would fain
Have called in further aid: in vain
He urged it.—' No; no :—APOZEM
' She liked: fhe was content with him.
' Others would but th' expence encreafe,
' In vain; fo pray'd to die in peace.'

 " *Die*,—faid you?—JUPITER forefend
" You fhould be near your latter end!
" No; MARIANNE: I truft that we
" Shall both live long, and happily."

           ' It

' It is impoffible to fay.
' I hope we fhall : perhaps we may.—
' But,—hem !—this teazing cough of mine
' Is fymptom fure of a decline.
' I ne'er, till now, knew RUSTIC HALL
' Unhealthy ; but, the Damps, this Fall,
' Have brought a fever on, and cough,
' I fear me, I fhall not fhake off,—
' *At home :*—perhaps, a Journey wou'd,
' If taken fpeedily, do good.'

" Think you fo, Love ? Heav'n grant it may !
" We 'll take a journey.   But, which way ?
" To DORSET's Downs ? Or, Hills of DEVON ?
" Or, further Weft, to CORNWALL even ?
" If not afraid to crofs the Seas,
" We 'll go to LISBON, if you pleafe :
" To NICE ; MADEIRA ;—any where
" To benefit you by the air."

' Now you outrun my hopes, my dear
' AGRESTIS.   We 'll not go fo far.
' A Journey only LONDON to,
' May all that we can wifh for do.
' We 'll leave our fogs, and cares behind,
' At RUSTIC HALL ; and chear our mind   }
' With all th' Amufements we can find.

' 'Twill

‘ ’Twill change the place, the fcene, the air—’ ⎫
“ No doubt of ’t.   Change of place, my Dear, ⎬
“ Will change the fcene, and eke the air.— ⎭
“ But I have never underftood,
“ That change from bad to worfe was good.”

‘ *Children*——though *you* no family
‘ Have had, nor opportunity
‘ To try th’ effect, yet might you know—
‘ How much to change of air they owe,
‘ In hooping-coughs’.

                     “ Not fuch, my Dear,
“ Is yours : although a Child you are :
“ Or would be treated like a Child ;
“ And with a LONDON Rattle fpoil’d.
    “ Nay, look not angry, MARIANNE :
“ I think, I ’m not a churlifh man :
“ Yet not fo facile, or fo fond,
“ To go difcretion’s bounds beyond.
“ I ’ve oft refufed to go to Town ;
“ Now, I confent : but I will own
“ Fairly the truth, I ’ve bufinefs there.
“ As to the *goodnefs* of its air
“ For Invalids,—or morals for
“ Perfons in health,—I do abhor
“ The thought of Town.   Nathlefs prepare
“ Your clothes : we ’ll pafs the winter there.”

                                    (To

(To cut off much as I am able
Of this already-tedious Fable.)
Fancy our Couple fafe arrived
In LONDON. Fancy they have lived
There long enough for MARIANNE
To have alarm'd her Gentleman.
With pain AGRESTIS faw his Wife
Give into fafhionable life.
Levity mark'd her conduct; which,
Though to a crime it might not reach,
Affected him. Like CÆSAR, he
Would not fhe fhould *fufpected* be.
Too intimate his Wife became
With LADY GADABOUT, a Dame
Of fafhion; of *notorious* fkill
At Cards; who oft'ner at Quadrille
Black Aces held,—and Pam at Loo,
Than fhe was thought entitled to.
Though high in rank, fhe kindly ftoop'd
To any one—that would be duped.
Squires' Dames but newly come to Town
She cull'd; and ' mark'd them for her own.'
With MARIANNE acquaintance made
At fome Affembly where they play'd
Together, LADY GADABOUT
Took care to have her at her rout:

Was

Was civil to excefs : fo much
. As ev'n to proffering her coach,
Or corner in it, to a Play,
Or Mafquerade, or Ranelagh ;
To Hyde-Park, or to Kenfington ;
Or *ſhopping* over all the Town.
She fwallowed greedily the bait :
In other words,—grew intimate.

  What not difpleafed her, MARIANNE
Ufually had fome Gentleman
To flirt with her.   New faces draw
Attention.   This AGRESTIS faw :
And jealous of a Hufband's honour,
Not only kept an eye upon her,
But gave her hints :—" That fuch a Dame,
" And fuch, (whofe conduct was the fame
" As MARIANNE's,) was much to blame."

  Madam their conduct juftified ;
And faid,—' The cruel world belied
' Women of worth : that, as to her,
' None durft impeach her character :
' But, if they did, her *virtuous* mind
' Scoff'd at the malice of mankind.'

  AGRESTIS knew that Women made
Then of their virtue moft parade

                                    When

When they were juſtly ſubject to
Suſpicion : but too much he knew,
An accuſation to advance
Without or proof, or circumſtance.

It is a curſe in caſes ſuch
To know too little, or too much.
When a Man knows the worſt, he may
Take comfort one or other way :
But, doubt, uncertainty, ſuſpenſe
Reſiſt the counſels of good ſenſe,
And reaſon : 'tis in vain we try
To practiſe then philoſophy.

Hearing that MARIANNE was gone
Airing one morn to Kenſington,
AGRESTIS tow'rd the Gardens bent
His ſteps. As through Hyde-Park he went,
He ſaw SIR FOPLING FLUTTER there,
Taking, with MARIANNE, the air :
Although he had forbidden her
Speaking to him ; whoſe character
Was infamous as Man's could be ;
Not for his feats of gallantry ;—
Thoſe the World doubted : but, his tongue
On Women's reputation hung,
Like Mildew : and once faſten'd on,
Blaſted the plant it fed upon.

X   AGRESTIS

AGRESTIS chofe not to intrude;
But fullenly his walk purfued.
Nor being in a humour fit
For any Friend that he might meet,
He fought an unfrequented part;
To vent the forrows of his heart.

There is, from public eyes remote,
And diftant from the Walks, a Spot
Delightful: water, wood, and lawn
In miniature; by nature drawn.
Art, too, has added an alcove,
Where happy People have made love ;—
And wretched made complaint ; in fcrawls
Ill-fpelt: as witnefs all the walls.
This liked AGRESTIS well. He fate
Revolving on the married ftate.
And, as he faw no Creature by,
Made a long, loud foliloquy
Againft the Sex.

                     When, lo! a MOLE,
That overheard him from its hole,
Uprear'd its head; and thus began:
' Why! what a fimpleton is Man!
' Tyrant Tormentor, to deny
' Women their ways of Gallantry!
' Is this the proof of human fenfe,—
' To look for female continence?

' By marriage bands to think to tie
' The Sex; and make them property?
' Why form connexions? Man may have
' Pleafure without. Why be a flave
' To his own notions too refined?
' What boots it to enjoy the *mind*?

 ' How much, much happier is a Brute;
' Who from mere appetite *goes to 't* : *
' Nor does who went before regard;
' Nor who directly afterward!'

 A BLACKBIRD lent unwilling ear,
So long; but would not longer hear.
The Libertine he thus reproves:
" Talk not of your inceftuous loves,
" Ye Moles; who, Father, Daughter, Mother
" And Son, hold commerce with each other.
" Nature, when fhe had form'd your race,
" Forefaw in you her own difgrace;
" And left your manners fhould be found,
" And follow'd, hid you under ground.
" But, that with lefs remorfe ye might
" Your lufts enjoy, your fole delight,
" Nature compaffionate and kind,
" To fpare your blufhes—ftruck you blind."

 The MOLE thus anfwer'd fneeringly:
' Ere BLACKBIRDS fpout philofophy,

       ' Better

   * S H A K S P.

' Better inftructed they fhould be.
' Fools only think we cannot fee.
' They are miftaken. MOLES have eyes;—
' But *wink* at female perfidies.——
' And fo would Men if they were wife.'.

AGRESTIS, who attentive fate
This while, forbade the MOLE to prate.
But earneftly the BIRD he pray'd
To talk with him the while he ftay'd.

The BLACKBIRD, of congenial mind
With his; of folitary kind;
Wary, and fhy; ftopp'd ne'erthelefs
To counfel him in his diftrefs.
  " I heard your long foliloquy;
  " And that vile Animal's reply.
  " As him I reprobated; you
  " I meant to counfel what to do.
  " Back to the Country quickly take
  " Your Wife: as yet, fhe 's but *a Rake*
  " *At heart:* *—another week, or two,
  " May make a *horned Beaft* of you.
  " Nor fhe alone to blame will be:
  " You give the opportunity.
    " Humanity to vice is prone:
  " Scarce to be trufted when alone;

" But

* P O P E.

" But more corrupt it grows ;—much worfe,
" By too familiar intercourfe.
" Shall Men in Cities pafs their lives,
" Exhibiting their handfome Wives
" To public gaze :—in wanton drefs
" At Balls ;—more wanton nakednefs
" At Mafquerades :—with wine inflame,
" And Dance :—yet think to keep them tame?
" When th' ebullition of the blood
" Takes place, will *preaching* do them good?
" O ! 'tis incongruous to fuppofe
" The Dame that much in public goes
" Can long be chafte. Or, hurry home,
" Or, bow your neck to Cuckoldom."

The BIRD's advice exactly hit
AGRESTIS' thoughts : it feem'd fo fit,
He was refolved to follow it.

A Chaife, next morning at the door
Betimes, reluctant MADAM bore
From PICCADILLY. As fhe paft
The PARK, a *lingering look* fhe caft;
And figh'd to think it was the laft.
As from the windows fhe withdrew
Her head, fhe dropt a tear or two :
Then fulking in the corner fate ;
Nor deign'd to look upon her mate,

Nor

Nor anfwer him.   At length, howe'er,
Silence fo grievous was to bear,
To " Yes,—and No " fhe condefcended;
Till, in due time, her fullens ended.

At RUSTIC HALL they fafe arrived:
Now their fole refidence.   They lived
On fo-fo terms : but grew more dear
Each other to, from year to year.
For Country air, and quietude
Gives even current to the blood.
And when the hey-day once was o'er,
MADAM—of LONDON thought no more;
But tafte for rural life acquired:
AGRESTIS loved: his ways admired.
He, on his part, with rapture fired
Anew, in her found all that he defired.

This happinefs they ne'er had known,
Had they lived one month more in TOWN.

FABLE

F A B L E XLVIII.

The INSECT NATURALIST.

IN queft of Objeƈts new, a GNAT
Obferved a TUMULUS, or Mount;
And, very anxious to know what
It might contain, alighted on 't.

As 'twas impoffible to look
Through fuch a vaft opacous mafs,
The curious Creature undertook
His weak probofcis through to pafs.

Day after day the tafk effay'd ;
His fpirit would not let him flinch;
By labour hard a hole he made,
In depth a quarter of an inch.

At length he found 'twas fruitlefs toil;
For, deeper not a line he went.
All he could do but ferved to fpoil
His little feeble inftrument.

Reluƈtant, then, he laid afide
The trial : but *Hypothefes*
A many form'd ; to fave his pride ;
And folve his own perplexities.

ARE

ARE not *Men* full as arrogant ?—
To futile Syſtems who give birth :
And not content to walk on, want
To penetrate into the EARTH ?

What matters whether *Water*, *Fire*,
Metal, or *Marble* 's at the Centre ?
HIS Works we ſhould with awe admire,
Into whoſe Secrets none can enter.

This Fable is not intended to reprefs that ardour of *philoſophic*
Enquiry, which, when it runs not counter to Religion, is the glory of
Man :—but it is meant to check, and at the ſame time to reprehend,
the *preſumption*, the *folly*, and the *wickedneſs* of thoſe, who by
calling in queſtion the truth of the MOSAIC SYSTEM, would
thereby weaken our religious Faith.

FABLE

F A B L E   XLIX.

The affected B E A R.

A BEAR obferved an Ape one day
  Making a troop of Females gay
By his pert nonfenfe, and grimaces.
So he muft do the fame, forfooth:
And made himfelf yet more uncouth
  By practifing—what he thought—*Graces.*

He learnt upon his toes to walk;
And fmirk'd, and fmil'd; and had fmall talk—
  As much as twenty Bears need have.
Yet more his gallantry to prove,
To every Female he made love;
  Was every one's " obfequious Slave."

At Routs, and Balls, he *fo* admired them,—
So complimented,—teafed,—and tired them,—
  At laft, one whifper'd in his ear;
' Friend BRUIN ;—no more bows, and fcrapes :
' *Coxcometry* is bad in *Apes,*—
  ' But worfe, believe me, in a *BEAR.*'

Y   *FABLE*

F A B L E L.

The Simple FARMER.

A Countryman of more conceit, than fenfe,
    Thought he could mend the ways of Providence:
And begg'd of Jupiter, to let his Corn
Grow without beard; for, once his hands were torn
In reaping it.   Jove granted his requeft.
The Corn fo grew.   The Countryman feem'd bleft.
The *Birds* were more fo : for, with little pain,
And with no rifk, they peck'd out every grain.
Their's was the Harveft.   And the Farmer found,
At Autumn, only Straw upon the ground.
On which, he doff'd his hat, and fcratch'd his head ;
And growing wifer by the leffon, faid,——
" I 'm rightly ferved.   Yet, gracious Jove, forgive
" My paft prefumption.   Let me hence receive
" Thy benefits, beftowed as heretofore ;——
" Or, *as to Thee feems meet.*   I afk no more."

F . A B L E   LI.

The EAGLE, the CROW, and the SHEPHERDS.

THE King of Birds, an Eagle, once
    Bore off a Lambkin in his pounce.
A CROW obferved the royal feat;
And had a mind to copy it.
He faw a Lamb; alighted on 't';
And fain aloft with it would· mount.
To take firm hold of it, the fool
His feet entangled in the wool.

  ' The SHEPHERDS faw; and came upon
Straightway and feized the Simpleton.
  Whilft they preparing were the knife
To take away his forfeit life;
The CROW befeech'd,—' They 'd let him loofe.
' Alleging truly in excufe,
' What he had feen the EAGLE do.'

  " Will *his* injuftice fanction you ?—
(They faid.)   Befides; you ought to die,
" Were 't only for your *idiocy.*
" Shall *Crows,*—fuch abject Creatures,—dare ⎫
" To put themfelves upon a par   ⎬
" With the firft Bird that flits in air?— ⎭

                        " With

" With Jove's vicegerent? Do not you
" Know, that thofe ftrong in power can do
" Acts that would ill become the weak?
" Compare your, talons, and your beak
" With his.   It is the fame with us
" Men.   Though alike facinorous,
" Bafe deeds by Peafant done, or King;
" Yet dares the Monarch many a thing—
" Which, if the hardy Peafant fhou'd,
" He muft atone for 't with his blood.
    " Thy Folly 's fuch, thou could'ft not thrive,
" If we would let thee longer live:
" Therefore no ftruggling; but fubmit:
" For die thou muft, *for want of Wit.*"

F A B L E   LII.

The S N A K E, *and* J U P I T E R.

A SNAKE, which Lads tormented oft, addrefs'd
His plaint to JOVE ; and pray'd to be redrefs'd.
' His Life had long become to him a load ;
(He faid :) ' he was afraid to ftir abroad ;
' Left he with Schoolboys mifchievous fhould meet.
' The cruel Urchins took delight to beat,
' And ufe him ill: with fticks the larger ones ;—
' The lefs affail'd him with a fhower of ftones.'

" And whofe fault is it ? (JUPITER replies.)
" In your own *Teeth* your proper vengeance lies.
" Had you, when firft ill-ufed, refented it,—
" No Boy had after rifk'd the being bit."

WHEN for a *Coward* any one is known,
In every company he 's put upon.
What makes his ftate ftill more accurft :—
Poltrons, in order to conceal
Their daftardy, will be the firft
To bully him, and ufe him ill.

F A B L E

F A B L E LIII.

The AUTHOR, *and his* YOUNG FRIEND.

A YOUTH, who went one day to fee
His *bookiſh* Coz, in London, faid,—
‘ You ’ve never half the Company
‘ With you, that has our Kinfman NED.

‘ Go to his Dinners when one will,
‘ Though age is coming on him faſt,
‘ His maxim is,—“‘ *The* PRESENT ;’”—ſtill ;
“‘ *I know no* FUTURE ;—*damn the* PAST.’” ·

‘ Regretting,—“‘ *Why is Life ſo ſhort !*’”
‘ Oneanſwer’d him,—“‘‘ THE NEXT IS LONG.’”ˢ
“‘ *Is it ?* (fays he) *I ’m ſorry for ’t.*——
“‘ *Come, Lads ;—a Sentiment, or Song.*

“‘ *Bring t’other Bottle :—Brandy bring.* ＊
“‘ *Make noiſe enough, my Lads ;—make fun.*
“‘ *They call me, jeeringly,—a King :—*
“‘ *I will, at leaſt, be* drunk † *as one.*’”

＊ A vulgar Parody on “‘ *Bring the flaſk ; and muſic bring.*’”

† ‘ *To be drunk as a King,*’—is a proverb, happily grown out
of date. We have not, for many Reigns, had a drunken Beaſt upon
the Throne.

Scandalous

" Scandalous !—You fhall go no more
" To fee him. Can he not forbear,
" One day ?—Not give his follies o'er ?
" Would he fpoil all who wfth him are ?"

' Truft me, dear Coz, I 'll never do
' As NED does : never copy him.
' But—pardon me ;—pray, do not you
' Live *t'other way* in the extreme ?

' Is 't right to be alone fo much ?
' But—you 're a Satirift, they fay.
' Many I know account you fuch.
' Have you not frighten'd folks away ?'

" You 've hit it. He who wields the pen
" Of Satire, muft give umbrage to
" The Fools and Rogues amongft the Men,
" And worthlefs Women not a few.

" But think not I 'm *alone,* my dear
", Coufin : behold where HOMER fits :—
" There JUVENAL :—and HORACE here :
" BUTLER, BOILEAU, and other Wits.

" You know their worth to eftimate :
" Is there not more in every page
" Of theirs, than in the idle prate,—
" The empty jargon of this Age ?"

FABLE

F A B L E   LIV.

The V I P E R, *the* F I L E, *and the* S M I T H.

——— *Fragili quærens illidere dentem*
Offendet folido.

HOR.

A VIPER crawling in a SMITH's Shop, found
A FILE of harden'd Steel upon the ground :
Which with accuftom'd malice as he bit,
The SMITH exclaims—' You 've furely loft your wit.*
' I 've feen you oft fuccefsfully at work
' On fuch foft, fpungy fubftances as Cork ;
' But, take my word for 't, you will only fpoil
' Your brittle teeth by gnawing at a FILE.'

* Αλλ' ευηϑης ει.

F A B L E

F A B L E LV.

NOVELTY, and COMMON-SENSE.

ON the fame fhelf perchance were found
Two BOOKS, ne'er meant to be together;
The ONE in humble fheepfkin bound;
T' OTHER in red Morocco leather.

The fpruce one, NOVELTY, began:—
' You-Sir! How dare you joftle me?
' Foregad, if I had my ratan,
' I'd make you quit my company.'

When COMMON-SENSE obferved who fpoke,—
A very Beau,—a *Thing*, fo kempt,
And drefs'd,—he darted him a look
Of moft ineffable contempt.

The Beau proceeded: ' Some one fetch
' Away this fellow. I am fick
' At feeing fuch a tatter'd wretch.
' Shopman, I fay, make hafte; be quick.'

" Ay: prithee, do; fays COMMON-SENSE.
" I'm weary of this Lordling's prate.
" Or him remove, or take me hence;
" Any thing fo we feparate."

Z   Juft

Juft then came in a Cuftomer;
Who taking two fuch Volumes down,
Call'd SHAFTSBURY a *Sophifter*;
And purchafed the *Logician* BROWN. *

* JOHN BROWH, M. A. who in 1751 publifhed fome admirable
ESSAYS on the CHARACTERISTICS.

F A B L E   LVI.

The F O X, *finding, a* M A S K.

A S RENARD ftroll'd abroad one day,
He found a VIZARD in his way.
' Pity! (fays he,) who took fuch pains
' To *paint* thee, could not give thee *Brains.*

RENARD perhaps would fay;—*The Fair*
Who paint their faces—brainlefs are.

FABLE

F A B L E LVII.

The SPIDER, and the WASP.

A SPIDER who his web had fpread
$\quad$ Some months, and caught a many flies,
By his fuccefs, at length, was led
$\quad$ To try to make a WASP his prize.

When he had ftrengthen'd, as he thought,
$\quad$ His work that nothing could break through,
The WASP,—fo far from being caught,—
$\quad$ Away with all the Tackling flew.

The SPIDER from its lurking hole
$\quad$ Obferved his unembarrafs'd flight;
Then curfed itfelf for Knave, and Fool;
$\quad$ Fretted; fell fick; and died with fpite.

THE *APPLICATION*, I 've not time,
$\quad$ Or am too idle, now to make;
Any one who can tag a rhime
$\quad$ May, in my ftead, that pleafure take.

$F A B L E$

F A B L E   LVIII.

The EAGLE, and the TORTOISE.

⁎ *I have told this Fable before:* (See page 78 : Fable xxvii :)
and drawn from it its obvious general *Moral. At present I de-*
duce from it a partial, *and seemingly a ludicrous one; but unhappily*
warranted by the Accident which befell ESCHYLUS, *the Dra-*
matiſt, and which coſt him his life.

AN EAGLE in his talons took
A TORTOISE, who *would ſee the World*;
But, when aloft, the Fool he hurl'd
Againſt the fragment of a Rock.

'Tis ſaid, The EAGLE threw him down
On a Man's head as bald as Stone ;—
Which he perchance miſtook for one.

Decapillated Beaus, take care :
Keep on your Hats abroad, or wear
Perriwigs, ye who have no hair.

Decapillated.]   I hope the Reader will accept of this new-coined
word, when I aſſure him I have been ſearching for a current phraſe
above five minutes without ſucceſs.

FABLE

F A B L E   LIX.

The LEOPARD, and the FOX.

⁎ *Looking back to the duplicate of the laſt* FABLE, *I obſerve, upon the ſame page this of the '* LEOPARD, and, the FOX,' *told in two lines only; and partaking of the* obſcureneſs *of* Brevity; *which, in Compoſitions of this kind, intended for the Young, as well as the Old, ought particularly to be avoided. I therefore tell the Fable over again, ſomewhat dilated.*

A LEOPARD boaſting his variety
 Of Spots, and Colours beauteous to the eye;
A Fox, who heard him, tauntingly replied:
" None will deny You have a fair *Outſide.*
" Your merit lies no deeper than your *ſkin:*
" Mine is intrinſic: I 've a *Mind* within."

F A B L E

F. A B L E. LX.

The Old-Woman, and the Cásk.

A Nurse, a perfect connoiſſeur in Gin,
  Found an old Keg with naught but dregs within.
Yet, to the bunghole ſhe her noſe applied,
And ſniffing ſtrongly as ſhe could, ſhe cried;
' Exquiſite ſmell!—But, oh! how exquiſite
' The *Liquor* muſt have been, whoſe very dregs delight.'

'TIS thought that Phædrus by this Fable wou'd
Hint his own *former* worth, who was ſo good
A Bard when old.   If I as old ſhould be,
And give the world my dregs of poeſy,—
I wiſh the Fable may as well ſuit me.

END OF THE FABLES.

INDEX.

I N D E X.

F   I   N   I   S.

uct-compliance